Wyoming Wedding

Book One in Culpepper Cowboys

by

Kirsten Osbourne

Wyoming Wedding

Book One in Culpepper Cowboys

by Kirsten Osbourne

Prologue

Karlan Culpepper leaned forward in his chair, resting his elbows on the kitchen table as he scrubbed his hands over his face. He looked at his brothers, all of whom looked as defeated as he felt. "Why would Grandpa do this to us?"

Cooper shrugged. "He's been on all of us to marry for the last five years. I don't think any of us should really be surprised by this."

"Well, I know! But to force us to marry? To keep the ranch we grew up on? There's no way I'm going to let Travis inherit it. He hated coming here even when we were kids. Remember? And no matter what, he's always going to get a tenth of the profits from the ranch, unless we sell. Like we'd ever sell! Of course, he could get a fifth of the profits if he worked with us, but we all know we'd rather he didn't work the ranch with us."

Kolby shook his head. "He always refused to help with chores. He spent all this time on his stupid Game Boy. He was afraid of horses!"

Karlan sighed. "Well, I really don't think we have a choice. The will said for the four of us to inherit this ranch, we need to all be married within a year. And one of us needs to have a wife who's knocked-up."

Their mother walked over and set drinks on the table for them. "Be a little less vulgar about it," Linda said as she walked away.

Karlan glared at his mother as she walked off. "One of our wives will need to be in the family way. Is that better, Mother?"

"Yes!"

Chris, the youngest of the four brothers, shook his head. "So how on earth are we going to find four women to move out here in the middle of nowhere and marry us? All the girls that were raised around here are married to those stupid underwear models."

All of the brothers knew what he was talking about. Two years before, some idiot had come up with the bright idea to shoot underwear advertisements at a neighboring ranch. When the girls in town had heard that there were hot male models running around in just their underwear, they all volunteered to help out. A freak spring blizzard had broken out, trapping everyone at the ranch, and there had been a lot of quick weddings after. And a whole lot of babies born nine months later.

Culpepper had always been a ranching community, so there weren't a whole lot of girls who stuck around anyway. They moved off somewhere where they could get a job. And now it seemed the ones who stayed married underwear models.

Karlan shrugged. "I guess we're going to have to join some kind of online dating service or something."

"No, it's going to have to be more severe than that. I think we're going to have to get a matchmaker involved. There aren't any girls anywhere close enough." Cooper look disgusted by the idea.

"A matchmaker? What year do you think this is?" Karlan asked sarcastically.

"I knew a guy in college, who I've kinda kept in touch with. A couple years ago, he did a website for this matchmaker woman, and she ended up matching him up with his wife. They've got a kid and they're really happy." Chris didn't look excited by the idea of seeing a matchmaker, but at least he seemed to feel like they could do it.

"Really? See if you can get her name for me. Wonder if we can just have her ship four girls out here and we can pick from them."

"I don't think she works that way. Trey said that she introduced them at the altar."

Kolby jumped to his feet. "No way. I'm not marrying some random stranger. I need to at least know if I like her first."

Karlan rubbed the back of his neck. "Chris, just get the number for me. I'll call her. I'll see what we can do." He really didn't want to do something so desperate, but he couldn't imagine living anywhere other than the ranch. Culpepper, Wyoming, was their home. They couldn't lose it.

Chapter One

Dr. Lachele Simpson got out of her rental SUV and pushed her purple hair back over her shoulder before walking up to the entrance of the large Wyoming ranch house. The door was opened before she had the chance to knock.

A middle-aged woman with short blond hair and green eyes opened the door. "Are you Dr. Simpson?"

Lachele nodded. "Yes. Please call me Dr. Lachele everyone does!"

"I'm Linda Culpepper." Her gaze went past Lachele's shoulder to the rental vehicle. "I can't believe you got a dented car for a rental!"

"Oh, it wasn't dented when I got into it. That happened because I was talking to the rental agency girl and backed into a pole in the parking garage at the airport. It's a good thing I always get the extra insurance!"

Linda simply nodded, opening the door wide to let Lachele into her home. "Do you have trouble with rental cars often?" Before closing the door, Linda looked once more at the dented car, shaking her head.

Dr. Lachele shrugged. "I tend to have trouble keeping dents off everything I drive. My husband just laughs. I never hurt myself, because they're always low-speed collisions because I'm not paying attention."

"Maybe you should start paying attention!"

"Oh, I'm sure I should. Will I? Probably not." Lachele looked around for the men she was there to see. "Are your sons here?"

"They're all out on the ranch. I'm supposed to text as soon as you get here, and they'll come right home. I'm sorry for the inconvenience, but they couldn't spend the day sitting around. There's always work to be done on a ranch." Linda led the way to the huge living area. "Can I get you anything to drink while you wait?"

Lachele nodded. "Sweet tea would be great if you have some."

"I do. I'm a Texas girl born and raised. We're required to have sweet tea at all times." Linda hurried to the kitchen to get two glasses of iced tea while Lachele sat down on the couch and waited.

Linda handed Lachele her glass and sat down opposite her. "Thank you for coming all this way. I know this isn't how you usually do things."

Lachele frowned. "It's not. I travel all the time to interview people. It's the idea of choosing four women for four men that's strange to me. Usually before I send a woman out, I have everything planned. I even help plan most of these weddings. I certainly don't leave the matchmaking to chance."

"But I'll be here supervising everything. There will be no

hanky-panky going on under my roof."

Lachele laughed. "More than anything, I want to make sure the girls are provided for. I'm here to interview your sons and put them through my rigorous testing, but before I even start that, we're going to get some ground rules set."

"That sounds fair to me. Do you want me around for this discussion? Or do you want me to make myself scarce?"

Lachele thought about that for a moment. "I think I want you to stay. I want you to know the rules that I'm giving the boys, so that you can help me enforce them. I have a feeling they listen to you."

"Not as much as I'd like." Linda frowned.

Lachele laughed. "I have a son too. I don't think they ever listen. Did you only have boys?"

"Yes, I always hoped for a daughter, but my husband died before I had any." Linda smiled. "I love my boys more than anything."

Lachele looked at her watch. "How long before the boys get here?"

Linda laughed. "They'd get here a lot quicker if I actually texted them." She pulled her phone from her pocket, and quickly texted them all. "So sorry about that. That's what happens when you're my age. Your mind starts to go."

"Oh, I know."

"I think it's the horrormones."

Lachele laughed. "That's gotta be it." She liked Linda. She had one of those personalities that everyone liked.

"Are you going to stay here while you're in town? Karlan told me the testing would take several days."

"I made a reservation at the hotel in town, but if you don't mind, I'll stay here. I drove past and it looked a little scary. I think you and I would make great friends."

"Oh, I know we would."

Both women turned and looked at the door when they heard it open. Lachele patted her chest as four sexy cowboys walked into the house. She looked at Linda. "You did *good*!"

Linda laughed. "I'm pretty proud of them."

As they filed into the room and sat down, Linda introduced each of them. She indicated each man as he sat down. "That's Karlan, he's my oldest. He's the mayor of Culpepper, as well as being in charge of this ranch. Next comes Cooper, he's more the foreman around here. Then we have Kolby. He's Cooper's right-hand man. And youngest is Chris. Chris is our black sheep. During the school year, he's a traveling science teacher. He goes to the different homeschool families and teaches chemistry and physics."

"And why does that make him a black sheep?" Lachele asked.

Karlan raised an eyebrow. "Because he's a science nerd instead of a rancher. He helps out around his other stuff."

Lachele grinned. She took a sip of her iced tea before starting the conversation she needed to have with the men. "Before I even start the testing, I want to make it clear that we'll be doing things my way. If I'm going to send girls out here to spend time with you, taking them away from their lives, I need a guarantee of marriage. I'm going to ask you all to sign a contract, that states if one of the women isn't married within a month of coming here, she shall be compensated ten-thousand dollars to start over somewhere else. Do any of you have any arguments with that?"

The men squirmed as they looked at each other. "I don't think so," Karlan said, the spokesman for the others. "According to Grandpa's will, we're required to get married within six months. And one of us has to have a wife who is expecting within a year."

Lachele jotted down a quick note. "So you need brides who are willing to have babies right off. I'll make sure of that with my questions to them. Second provision is that you have to stay together for one year. I'd rather you let me choose which bride is for each of you, but I won't require that."

Karlan frowned. "I know that's how you usually do business. I appreciate you making an exception for us. Is there anything else we need to know before we get started on the testing?"

"No. Those are the only special rules I am making for you. I do want to make sure that the girls stay in this house with your mother until you are married. Don't you boys be trying to lure those girls back to your own houses." She'd been told from the beginning that each of the men had their own house on the ranch.

"No, ma'am. We're too afraid of our mama for that."

"You sound like smart men. So, who wants to be tested first?"

"I'll go first. I'm the oldest, so I'll be the guinea pig." Karlan got to his feet. "Do you want to do it here? Or back at my place?"

Lachele looked at Linda. "Do you mind if we do it here?"

Linda shook her head. "Not at all. Why don't you two work here in the living room, and I'll go get started making lunch. The rest of you boys can scatter. Come back in an hour for lunch."

Lachele watched as the younger three boys followed their mother's orders. She liked this family already.

*****

Lachele checked into the hotel the girls had told her she should go to. She wasn't sure why they wanted her to meet them in a hotel rather than in their home, but she was willing.

Her cell phone rang as she walked into her room. She didn't bother to check the number as she swept her finger across the screen and put the phone to her ear. "This is Lachele."

"This is Hope Quinlan. Are you here?"

"Yes, I'm on the third floor in three-fifty-two. I have a suite, so come on up."

She pulled her suitcase into the bedroom, and closed the door. The suite was huge. There were two bedrooms and a large sitting area. There was even a small kitchen. It would be the perfect place for her to entertain the sisters while she put them through her rigorous testing.

She put the drinks and snacks she'd purchased away and walked to the door of the suite. She opened it and saw four young ladies, the one in front with her hand ready to knock.

"You must be the Quinlan sisters. I'm Dr. Lachele."

The girl in the front, a pretty, slim, blonde smiled. "I'm Hope."

Lachele opened the door wide. "Come in. I can't wait to get started." The girls filed into the room. "Have a seat. Do you want anything to drink?"

Hope, who seemed to be the spokesperson for all of them, shook her head. "We just stopped and got something to eat about an hour ago. I think we're all set for a while."

Lachele sat down in a big, comfortable chair. "Well let's get down to business then. Tell me why you're interested in finding men this way."

Hope exchanged looks with her sisters. "Let me start by introducing everyone. This is my sister Joy, that is Faith, and over there is Chastity." She pointed to each sister as she spoke. "We're something of a novelty in our town. We're the only quadruplets who have ever lived there."

Lachele frowned. "And you want to get away from being famous?"

Joy shrugged. "In a way. We live in a tiny, little town. We can't blow our noses without someone telling our parents about it. There are six girls in our family, and we all have these ridiculous names. It's like we're part of the trick pony show. We're expected to march in every parade. And none of us are allowed to get jobs. Our father thinks that would make us unladylike."

"We all have college degrees, but we're not allowed to use them. Our father said the only thing we were allowed to get degrees in was homemaking. Mama called it getting our MRS." Hope crossed her ankles and folded her hands in her lap.

Lachele frowned. "But you're not allowed to work?"

"Of course not. Daddy says he makes enough money that none of us should ever work. Our jobs are finding husbands. He doesn't realize that all the boys in town think of us as such an oddity that nobody's willing to ever ask us out. Not that he'd let us go. We're supposed to find husbands, who are willing to court us, not date us, and are willing to do all of this under his watchful eye." Hope shrugged.

"And how do *you* feel about that?"

Joy shook her head. "We all want to be independent. We've just never been allowed to be. That's why we want to get away more than anything. We want to be able to live our lives the way we want to live. Not constantly under someone else's scrutiny."

Lachele nodded. "I can understand that. How do you feel about having children right away?"

Hope smiled. "I love kids. I want at least a dozen. If I could have one in my arms tomorrow, I'd be thrilled."

"Okay, good. The men I have in mind for you four are asking for something different than I've ever done. They want me to send four women, and then they would be able to choose from the women sent. I'm making special provisions for this. The four of you would live with their mother. They'd be required to marry you within a month or they would have to pay you ten-thousand dollars apiece for relocation costs. There would be my normal contract to sign that requires you to stay together for at least a year."

The sisters exchanged looks. Finally, Chastity asked, "What if they want some of us and not all of us?"

"Then some of you marry and some of you won't. Is that a problem?"

Chastity shrugged. "I guess not. We've never really been separated before."

Faith frowned. "I can't imagine some of us staying there and some of us moving away."

Lachele looked between them. "Well, if two of you end up marrying the brothers, the other two would have twenty thousand dollars. You could put down roots right there in town and marry someone else there, still staying close."

That seemed to relieve all of them. "So how do we get started?" Hope asked nervously.

"I'll interview each of you. The tests take hours. Are you all staying the night here in the hotel?"

"Yes, ma'am," Hope replied. "Our parents know we're here in Paducah for the weekend. We told them we were going to the wedding of a college friend and needed to stay in town."

"So you're hiding this from your parents?" Lachele wasn't sure how she felt about that.

"For now we are," Joy told her. "If we end up going, we'll tell them. If you knew our parents, you'd understand."

Lachele shrugged. "Your lives. Who wants to go first?"

Hope raised a hand. “I will. This is scary enough as it is. I should go first, so my sisters will know it’s okay.”

Lachele smiled. “I promise, it’s not that rough. I’m just going to ask questions. I want to make sure I feel like you’re each right for one of the brothers.”

Joy leaned forward. “What do you want us to do? Should we leave?”

Lachele shrugged. “I’ll be taking turns asking all of you questions for a while. I’d rather you stuck close. Is there shopping you'd like to do close by? Or you could always go hang out in your room or watch the boob tube in one of the bedrooms."

Faith stood up. "There's a doll shop near here that I want to wander around in. They have some cute furniture."

Joy and Chastity jumped up to walk with their sister. "We'll be back before too long," Chastity said. "We just love looking at dolls."

When the three had left, Lachele looked at Hope. "Your sisters are odd."

"How do you think they'd be with our parents? It hasn't been easy growing up with absolutely no freedom. Here we are, twenty-two years old, and I think Chastity is the only one of us who has ever even kissed a boy. Well, Faith may have. She's hard to read sometimes."

Lachele made a quick note on her pad. "So tell me, why do *you* want to marry?"

Hope sighed. "I don't want to spend the rest of my life alone, and that's where I'm headed if I don't get out of town. My parents are going to keep us in a gilded cage forever. I'm not letting that happen."

Lachele smiled and patted Hope's hand. "Don't give up hope. Or should that be, 'Don't give up, Hope'? Either way I guess!" Lachele cackled softly at her own joke.

Hope just shook her head. She was used to jokes about her ridiculous name. If she had been the only one with a name like that, it would have been no big deal. She was just glad their mother hadn't had more daughters. Why, Patience and Charity would have been entirely too much!

*****

Karlan pulled his gelding, Mr. Ed, to a stop when he heard his cell phone ring. "Culpepper."

"Mr. Culpepper, this is Lachele Simpson."

He took off his black hat and toweled the sweat seeping down his chest. It was an unusually hot day for April. "Tell me you have good news for us, Dr. Lachele!"

"I do." Lachele laughed at that. "I sound like I'm the one getting married instead of you and your brothers."

Karlan rolled his eyes. "You sure do." Maybe if he humored the woman, she would answer his questions.

"I found four sisters who are willing to move to Culpepper as your brides."

He swallowed hard. As much as it was what he wanted, he couldn't believe she'd actually done it. "Sounds good. When will they be arriving?"

"They'll all be there a week from Saturday. They'll be driving out together."

"I'll let the others know. Mom will be thrilled to have other women around."

"I'm sure she will. I'll be there Saturday as well to introduce you all, but I'll rent a car and drive in from the airport. I want to make sure the first time you meet goes smoothly." Dr. Lachele paused for a moment. "You know what? I'll be there Friday. Tell Linda I'd like to stay with her again. If that's a problem, have her give me a call. She has my number."

"Yes, ma'am. I'll let her know. Thank you."

"Remember, you all have to be married within a month, or you settle ten thousand dollars on every unmarried sister."

Karlan closed his eyes for a moment. "I couldn't forget that." He ended the call and rode out to where his brothers were working together to repair a fence on one of their biggest pastures.

Cooper looked up from twisting some barbed wire fence around a nail, his thick gloves protecting his hands. "You're late." They'd all agreed to be back at one to finish the fence.

Karlan wanted to retort that they'd all been late a time or two, but with Cooper, it just wasn't true. He was never late for anything. "I got a call about that stoplight some folks are wanting to put in on Main St. Half the city council thinks it's a great idea and the other half is dead-set against it. Then, as I was riding back, I got a call from Dr. Lachele." He waited as all six eyes from his brothers landed on him. "Yeah, that Dr. Lachele."

Kolby glared. "Why are you making us wait? Did she find someone?"

"She found four sisters. They'll be here a week from Saturday. And Dr. Lachele is coming back to stay with Mom on Friday."

"Why's she coming back?" Chris asked. Chris wasn't actually allowed to help with any of the physical work, but they let him hand them nails and stuff. He just got in the way otherwise.

Karlan shrugged. "She said she wants to be here when we meet the women." He rubbed the back of his neck nervously. "I'm not sure I'm ready to meet someone and marry her that fast."

Kolby shrugged. "It's just marriage. We marry them. We have sex with them. We have babies. Will is fulfilled."

Karlan shook his head. "Women are always so much more than you give them credit for, little brother."

Cooper frowned. "They're going to get us all off schedule. You know they will."

Chris clapped Cooper on his back. "Something needs to get you off-schedule. Better a woman than anything else." It was Monday, and a school holiday, so he was home helping his brothers. He worked every day the school calendar called for, even though he only worked for homeschooled families. For some strange reason, the homeschooled families in the area always followed the school calendar. None of them understood it, but they accepted it.

Karlan sighed. "Let's get this fence done. I'm going to text Mom really quick and let her know we'll all be there for dinner. She needs to know the girls are coming. She's going to want to change the sheets."

"No one's slept on them since she changed them last!" Kolby protested.

"Like that's going to matter to Mom. These are her future daughters-in-law. She's going to welcome them with open arms."

"Aren't women supposed to hate their daughters-in-law?" Chris asked.

"We're talking about Mom. She'll make them all quilts and welcome them into the family." Karlan shook his head. Their mother was going to be so happy to not be the only woman on the ranch, she wasn't going to be able to contain herself.

They worked together through the afternoon with a minimum of words, each brother thinking about the woman he'd be marrying. Karlan thought maybe they'd have been smarter to let Dr. Lachele pair them off. She was the expert, after all.

Chapter Two

Hope was tired of her sisters. Well, only the ones that were with her. She wanted to pull her Chevy Equinox over to the side of the road and insist all three of them get out of the car. "I need to pee," Chastity said for the fiftieth time since they'd left the hotel that morning.

"I said we'd stop as soon as I see a place worth stopping. Do you want to go in a field?" Hope asked, the edge in her voice more obvious than she would like. "Why didn't you go before we left when I said to go?"

"I didn't have to go then. I need to go now!" Chastity complained.

Hope spotted a tiny gas station off to the right and pulled in. "Here you go. I hope they've cleaned that thing in the last fifteen years."

"At this point, I just can't care!" Chastity yelled as she wrenched the door open and ran for the station to get a key.

Hope leaned forward to rest her head on the steering wheel. It was their third day on the road, and they were only about a hundred miles from their destination. According to the GPS, they'd be there before lunch time. Well, if Chastity didn't keep making them stop.

"Do you want me to drive?" Joy asked, her voice soft and understanding.

Hope shook her head. "I've got it. I'll do better driving, because then I can't safely wrap my hands around Chastity's neck."

Faith sighed. "At least you don't have to sit in the backseat with her."

"Listening to the two of you argue is making me crazy," Hope said. "Please don't touch her again or do anything that will set her off. I need to feel sane when we arrive and meet the men."

"Did you say Dr. Lachele will be there when we arrive?" Joy asked, trying to change the subject smoothly.

Hope nodded. "She said she would be. She said something about becoming good friends with the men's mother."

"It's all going to be all right," Faith said softly. "Sorry about the bickering. I think we're all ready to be done with this car and meet the men. It's nerve wracking sitting back here, wondering when we'll meet the men of our dreams."

"I understand," Hope muttered. "I'm just tired, and we're all tense."

Chastity opened the door. "That bathroom was disgusting. I had to make a seat out of toilet paper, because my butt was not going to touch that gross potty."

Hope looked over at Joy and then into the rearview mirror at Faith. "I'm not stopping again. If anyone needs a drink, a snack, a toilet, now is the time. I swear, if I'm asked to pull over again, I might just hurt someone."

"I'm going to go get a couple bottles of water then," Chastity said, reaching for the door handle.

"No!" Faith and Joy yelled at the same time.

Joy was quick and locked the doors so no one could get out. "Go, Hope. If she gets water, she's going to need to pee in three minutes, and we're all going to end up in jail for sororicide."

Hope stepped on the gas, peeling out of the gravel parking lot much quicker than she should have. She didn't say a word as she pulled back onto the two-lane highway and pointed the car toward Culpepper. If they didn't reach the ranch soon, and she didn't get away from all of her sisters, but especially Chastity, she would hurt someone. It was not a good situation.

As they drove, Joy talked quietly, trying to keep everyone calm. She'd always been the peacemaker among them. "I hope my yarn gets there this week. Are the twins sending your kiln?" she asked Faith.

When they'd agreed to move to Wyoming, they'd had just under a week to pack everything they could. Every day, the twins would distract their mother while their older sisters would sneak away to the post office with packages they mailed to themselves in Wyoming. They'd spent thousands on mailing things, and they had been careful not to mail anything that would seem to be missing. It was crazy they had to sneak away at twenty-two years old, but what could they do?

Faith was a doll sculptor, and had begun a business that no one really knew about. Well, no one except them and a few others. They'd had to keep their business a secret from their parents, which was one of the reasons they wanted out of Kentucky. "Yeah, they're supposed to ship the kiln soon. I can't wait 'til I have my own workspace set up." Her voice sounded sad at the words, which surprised Hope. Faith loved her work.

"I'm expecting my yarn soon. I shipped it before we left. I'm glad we were able to bring your sewing machine, Hope." Joy sounded excited. "I brought along enough of my yarn and plastic canvas for a few rooms full of furniture." She made plastic canvas Barbie Doll furniture, and she had for years. She'd always found some little girl to give it to, but she'd always thought she could make a killing if she did it for a living.

Hope nodded. "I was thinking of making a selection of outfits that could be purchased separately from the baby dolls. I would have a little orange pumpkin outfit for Halloween, complete with an orange and green stem hat. I would do a red and white Santa outfit for Christmas. A bunny outfit for Easter. A green outfit with a Leprechaun hat for St. Patrick's Day. I think it could be a lot of fun."

Faith leaned forward, excited. "That sounds incredible. How much do you think it would cost to buy enough fabric to make all of those outfits?"

Hope thought for a moment. "Well, I'd buy each fabric in bulk, of course. We're probably looking at the outfits costing us about two or three dollars each. I think a set of six would be sold together."

"We could sell them for about sixty dollars? Do you think?" Faith asked. As always, when she thought about her doll business, she got very excited.

Hope nodded. She was the money girl. She was the only one of the six of them that could understand a spreadsheet without bursting into tears. "I think that would be good. I could crank them out pretty quickly after the first set."

"I think that's brilliant. I just wish Honor was here to make the cradles." Faith's voice was filled with sadness.

Chastity frowned. "We're going to have to find a way for Honor and Grace to join us here. Surely there are other men in town who need brides."

Hope sighed. As annoyed as she was with her sisters, the six of them had always been a unit. "We need to get them out from under Mom and Dad's rule."

"I wonder how mad they were when Grace gave them our letter?" Hope said, a frown on her face. "Has anyone talked to her yet?"

"I talked to her last night," Chastity said. "She said they were mad, but glad we were finally getting married. She was told to remind us not to let them kiss us before the wedding."

Hope rolled her eyes. "If I'm going to think about marrying someone, I'm going to kiss him. What if he drools?"

Chastity sighed contentedly. "Just think. In another month, none of us will be virgins. Sex, sex, sex."

Hope tuned the others out at those words. Chastity was off on her favorite subject as usual, and she had no desire to listen to her sex-crazed sister.

An hour later, Hope turned the car into a long driveway at a sign that read, "Culpepper Ranch." She smiled to herself. In a month, or hopefully sooner, she'd be married to one of the Culpepper Cowboys. Her heart beat faster as she realized she was minutes from meeting her future husband.

Stopping the car in front of the large white house, she put it into park. She stared at the house for a moment, wondering if they'd all lost their minds.

It didn't take a minute for the front door to burst open, and Dr. Lachele rushed out of the house, an older blond woman behind her. Hope took a deep breath and got out of the SUV, thrilled to be able to finally stand up. She rushed forward to hug Dr. Lachele.

"Hope, it's great to see you again," Dr. Lachele said, hugging Hope tightly. "This is my friend, Linda Culpepper. She's going to be your mother-in-law."

Hope was almost afraid to meet the woman. There were so many bad stories circulating about mothers-in-law, and Hope hadn't exactly had an easy time with mother figures anyway. "It's nice to meet you, Mrs. Culpepper."

The blond woman shook her head, reaching out to hug Hope. "Call me Linda."

One by one, Lachele introduced the other three sisters to Linda. "I just texted Karlan so the boys can come in for lunch and meet you ladies."

"Are they working today?" Hope asked, pushing her shoulder length blond hair back from her face.

Linda nodded. "They're always working. It's part of owning a ranch. You'll learn."

"I see." Hope opened up the hatchback of the vehicle and started to grab her bags.

"Leave them. You've driven too far to carry your own bags in. Besides, my boys have manners, and they'll do it as soon as they get here." Linda linked her arms with Hope and Faith, walking toward the house with them. "You girls are going to stay with me in the big house until the weddings happen. I hope you'll each find one of my boys to be perfect for you."

"I have suggestions for each of you if you want to hear them," Dr. Lachele told them.

Hope looked at the psychologist with surprise. "You do?"

Dr. Lachele nodded. "I have one of the men in mind for each of you. Would you like to know the one I think you should marry?"

Hope nodded. "I would!" She wished the matchmaker had set things up the way she usually did. She didn't want to have to go through the initial meeting and feeling uncomfortable stage. Maybe she was crazy, but she liked the idea of meeting at the altar.

"We'll talk after lunch then. I want all of you to meet all four of them, before I taint your mind with my opinions."

Hope sighed. "Yes, ma'am." She looked at Linda. "How can we help with lunch?"

Linda shook her head. "You've been driving for three days. You girls need to take a minute to just decompress before my boys are all forced on you." She led them to the living room. "You can wait here or there's a big back porch, if you'd prefer."

Hope smiled. "I like the idea of the back porch, but before I go, may I ask you one question?"

Linda nodded. "Sure."

"Where are you from? Your voice doesn't sound like Wyoming to me."

"Oh, I'm from Wiggieville, Texas. I moved here after the boys' father died to keep house for my father-in-law."

"Wiggieville? That's a strange name for a town!"

Linda laughed. "Actually it was named after one of my ancestors. I'll tell you the whole story later. I've always thought I wanted my grandma name to be Wiggie."

Hope tilted her head to one side. "Wiggie? Well, it's different, but if that's what you want, I don't see why not!" Hope walked toward the back door Linda had indicated, needing a few minutes in the quiet of the countryside.

She found a wooden porch swing off to one side, and she sank into it, staring out at the vast expanse of open land. She wondered how far the Culpepper ranch extended. Would this place really be her home for the rest of her life?

She leaned her head back and closed her eyes, listening to the quiet country sounds. She could hear a cow mooing in the distance, crickets chirping, birds singing softly to one another. Why, she could even hear the quiet bocking of chickens.

After a moment the sound of horse's hooves riding toward her and then stopping filled the air. She slowly opened her eyes to see a man throw his leg over the side of his horse and dismount, tying off his reins on the porch. "Hi."

Hope stared at him, her heart jumping into her throat. Never had she reacted so strongly to a man at first meeting. She laughed to herself softly. The truth was, she'd never reacted strongly to a man at all. She wasn't sure she possessed the type of emotions that it took for love, but she hoped she did.

"Hi. I'm Hope."

"I'm Karlan. I'm the oldest of the four brothers. Mayor of Culpepper, Wyoming."

"I'm Hope Quinlan. Oldest of the Quinlan quadruplets." Hope made a face. She hated being a quad. Why had she introduced herself that way?

"Wait. I knew we were marrying sisters, but quadruplets? Really?" Karlan walked over and sank down onto the swing beside her, setting the swing into motion with the kick of his boot.

"Really. And our names are god-awful too. I'm Hope, and my sisters are Faith, Joy, and Chastity."

"Is she really?"

"Is who really what?"

"Is Chastity really chaste?"

Hope laughed. "I sure wouldn't swear to it. That girl is—well, you'll see in a minute or two."

Karlan looked down at the pretty girl beside him. She was wearing a jean skirt and a long buttoned up shirt which was untucked. Her hair was shoulder length, which to him was the only thing that kept her from looking like a Bible thumper. "I'm not sure I care too much about meeting her. I think I've found my prize already."

Karlan was shocked to hear the words come out of his mouth.

He'd never come on so strongly with a woman, but he'd also never met one and felt his ding-a-ling immediately jump in his pants. Why he felt so much after a moment's acquaintance, he wasn't sure. Would he feel the same for her sisters? Were they identical?

"You may not think that after you meet the others. There are four of us after all."

"And four of us. Are you identical?"

She shook her head. "No. Thank God! We look like we're sisters, for sure, but we're easily told apart. We have younger sisters who are twins, and they're fraternal as well." She was certain she was babbling, but she'd never been left alone with a man before, and especially not one who made her feel *things*.

Karlan studied her face, glad they were close enough that he could see the small flecks of brown in her green eyes. "May I kiss you?"

Hope blinked a few times, surprised that he would ask that so soon after meeting. "I don't know. Do you think that would be right? Would it be weird if I ended up marrying one of your brothers, and you married one of my sisters and we'd kissed?"

He grinned. "No, but I don't plan on marrying anyone but you, darlin'." He leaned forward and gently brushed his lips against hers. His hand moved to cup her cheek.

Hope felt the passion shoot through her into her belly. She let out a gasp, and parted her lips, kissing him back. She'd always hoped it was possible for her to have these feelings for a man, and now here she was, enjoying a kiss.

She scooted closer to him, her hand going to the back of his neck. His tongue traced her lip, and she sighed happily. Her hand stroked the strong muscles of his neck, and moved down to his shoulders. This wasn't a man who sat behind a desk pushing papers around all day. This was a real man. It was all she could do not to climb onto his lap.

Karlan lifted his head, tapping her on the nose with his index finger. "Marry me. I'm staking my claim before my brothers see you."

"I—uh—we haven't known each other for five minutes."

"Hope, you just drove thirteen hundred miles to marry one of four strangers. Let it be me."

Hope slowly nodded, a smile creeping across her face. "Yes, I'll marry you." She wasn't certain why she felt so shy as she said it, but she did. She was glad she'd finished her wedding dress before leaving Kentucky. They could get married as soon as Wyoming laws would allow.

Karlan grinned, hugging her to him. "Let's go tell the others."

"Shouldn't we wait until tonight or something?"

"Why? You've agreed to be mine, and I'm ready to shout it from the rooftops." He wasn't even sure why he was so drawn to her, but he was. He wanted this one, not one of her sisters. Hope, well, she gave him hope. Hope for their ranch, and hope for his future. He could imagine spending long winter nights making love with her in front of a fire. Yeah, she was definitely the girl he'd been looking for.

Hope nodded slowly, not sure if her sisters would be angry

that she'd already gotten engaged to one of them before they even had a chance to meet him. She was used to being a self-sacrificing woman, so it felt weird not to let her sisters choose, and she would take the runt of the litter. Oh, she wanted him though.

Karlan stood and held a hand down for Hope, keeping her hand in his as they walked in through the backdoor of his mother's house. As soon as he'd closed the door behind him, he announced, "I'm marrying Hope."

Linda looked up from the ham she was carving. "Well, that was quick. Why am I not surprised?" She hurried around the counter and hugged Hope. "Welcome to the family!"

Hope felt her sisters' stares, and for a moment thought about apologizing. Why should she? It wasn't her fault that Karlan had seen her and immediately wanted to marry her. She had a right to be happy, didn't she?

Karlan was still holding Hope's hand, and as soon as his mother released her, he brought it to his lips.

Dr. Lachele hurried over to them, a big grin on her face. "I would have put you two together. There's no waiting period for a wedding in Wyoming."

Hope felt as if her heart was about to beat out of her chest. No waiting period? "Not even three days?"

"There's no waiting period in Kentucky, either," Joy reminded her.

Hope felt like the world was spinning out of control. She turned to Karlan. "So, we'll get married in three weeks or so?" That seemed like a reasonable period of time to wait. After all, her first kiss had been just minutes before.

Karlan shook his head, a smile touching his lips. "Today. That way you don't have to unpack more than once."

She put her hand to her throat. "Today?" she squeaked out.

Karlan nodded slowly. "Why wait? You came here to marry one of us."

Hope pulled him toward the back door. She had to talk through this, or she was going to have a panic attack right there in front of everyone. She hated when that happened. Once the door was closed, she turned to him, struggling for the right words.

"I did agree to marry one of you upon my arrival, but I thought I'd have a little more time to get to know you first. My first kiss was with you ten minutes ago. I can't—well, you know."

He shook his head, being deliberately obtuse. "No, I don't know. What can't you do?"

She closed her eyes, saying a silent prayer for help. "I can't sleep with a man I don't know. I need a couple of weeks before I'm ready for that."

He chuckled. "I can give you some time. I just want to get that knot tied nice and tight before any of my brothers get the chance to know you a little better."

Hope couldn't believe her ears. She opened one eye to see if he was serious. "Really? You'll give me time?"

Karlan used the hand he still held to pull her toward him. "Absolutely. I just like the idea of you living with me. I have three bedrooms. We don't even have to share a bed to start with. I don't want to have to play the courting game under Mom's watchful eyes, though. If we decide we're ready, we won't have to rush for the preacher, because we'll already be man and wife." And besides, he was pretty sure he could talk her into his bed within a couple of days, if not that night.

Hope nodded slowly. "Let's get married today then. I'd like a church wedding. Or at least to get married by a pastor."

"Our pastor from town will do it." He looked into her eyes, thinking. "How would you feel about getting married right here in my mom's backyard? I'd love to marry here on the ranch."

She nodded slowly. She had her wedding dress after all. "Later this afternoon?" It was just after noon. If they married around four, she'd have time to shower and get ready.

"Sounds perfect. Let me call Brother Anthony." Karlan watched her sit back down on the porch swing as he pulled out his phone, dialing the pastor of his church. He had the man on speed dial, because Cooper had insisted they all put him on speed dial before the women arrived. He didn't want anything to slow down their weddings.

"Brother Anthony. Karlan Culpepper. Are you free this afternoon?" After a three-minute conversation that made Karlan's head spin, he had the man agreeing to be there at four for a wedding. "Yes, of course, you can bring your wife. Miss Lovanne is always welcome!"

He clicked off the phone and took her hand pulling her to her feet. "You ready for this?"

Hope shook her head emphatically. "Of course not! But I'll manage." She stood on her toes and brushed her lips against his.

"I am happy I'm marrying you."

Karlan grinned. "Me, too. Let's go eat lunch!"

He took her hand and pulled her back into the house, thinking about kissing her later and not having to stop. Well, not unless she put the brakes on things, and he was pretty certain he could convince her that she'd look great wearing nothing but him.

Every eye was on them as they stepped into the room. Hope saw that her sisters had seemed to pair off with the Culpepper men. Chastity was trailing her fingers up and down someone's arm as if she wanted to drag him off to the bedroom and have her way with him. Hope said a quick prayer that her sister would hold off until after their vows were spoken. Or if she didn't, that she would pretend to hold off. If her sister was going to screw the man before the wedding, she didn't want to know about it.

Karlan took advantage of everyone's attention. "I just talked to Brother Anthony, and we're getting married this afternoon at four. I hope you'll all attend." The last was said with an impish grin.

"Today?" Linda asked, her voice full of surprise. "But how can you have a reception if you do it today?"

"Why don't we do a joint reception for all four couples after the last one gets married?" Karlan asked. "It'll save money and time. We can't all afford to take off a full day every week for a month."

Linda threw her hands up. "The ranch is the most important thing in the world. Don't worry. I won't forget again!"

Hope suddenly felt at home. The sarcasm, which had never

been apparent in her parents' house in Kentucky, warmed her from the insides. How could it not? She knew then she'd made the right decision by coming here, and by agreeing to marry the man beside her. She squeezed his hand, hoping he'd understand her silent communication.

Chapter Three

Linda volunteered her room for the girls to get ready in. It had a huge master bath that was perfect for the four girls, who were helped by Lachele.

Hope shivered as her sisters helped her slip her wedding dress over her head. She'd chosen this dress for a faceless man, who was so much more than she'd expected. All of the Culpepper men were huge, strapping cowboy-types. But Karlan in her mind, was the biggest, the strongest, the smartest, and the most handsome, all at once.

Linda was off helping the boys ready themselves, which made Hope sad. She would have liked to pepper her with questions about her oldest son.

"He's the one I would have chosen for you," Lachele said softly. "You picked well."

Hope smiled at that. "He just seems right. When he sat down beside me, I felt more for him than I've ever felt for another man." She didn't add that she'd spent her entire life thinking she was frigid. That she'd never feel the sexual excitement for a man she should.

Chastity sighed. "I can't believe you get to have *sex* tonight. I wish it was me."

Hope looked at her sister. “You want to have sex with Karlan?”

“Well, he’d do, but I’d sure prefer Chris. Have you seen that man? The sexiest of all of our Culpepper Cowboys.” Chastity had a faraway look on her face.

“Don’t sneak away to have sex with him, Chastity. Wait ‘til you’re married. Please.”

Lachele grinned as she observed the four sisters. Chastity sat on the bed mooning over Chris, a man she’d known for merely hours. Hope was in her wedding dress, looking more nervous than she’d ever seen a bride look. Faith was calm as she calmly did Hope’s make-up, as if she were working on one of her doll’s faces. Joy was detached, observing the others as if she felt as if she’d need to jump in to referee at any moment. The Culpepper Cowboys didn’t know what they were in for.

*****

“Why are you in such a hurry to marry her, Karlan?” Kolby asked. “You’d think you’d want to get to know her a little bit first.”

Karlan shrugged, not wanting to admit that he was trying to take her out of the running so none of his brothers could get to know her before she was married to him. “She seems like the right one for me. Why wait?”

Chris frowned. “I think Chastity’s the one for me, but I’m not marrying her today. No, sirree. I’ll wait as long as I can to make sure she’s just right.”

Kolby shrugged. “I think I want to marry Joy, but I want to

spend a little time with all of them first, just to be sure. Joy is tugging at me, but they're all gorgeous. Why should I pick today?"

Linda shook her head at them all, pinning sticky geraniums to each of their lapels. "If you'd let me have even a day's notice, we could have had carnations."

Karlan shook his head. "Does it matter what kind of flower we have?"

"Carnations are more traditional. They'd have looked better."

Cooper shook his head. "I think this makes their wedding unique. When I marry Faith, we'll have carnations, so you can get your carnation wedding in. Don't worry about that, Mom."

Linda looked at Karlan. "Speaking of which, she's not going to have a bouquet to carry. You need to pick her flowers on the way back to my house, so she can make a bouquet of them."

Karlan rubbed the back of his neck, wishing the wedding were over with. "Yeah, I'll do it."

They were in Karlan's living room, putting the finishing touches on their looks. All four men were freshly showered and wearing dark suits. Linda looked around at her four tall, handsome sons and sighed. "I wish your dad were here to see you now."

Karlan had few memories of his father, who had died when he was six. "I wish he was too." Truthfully, their granddaddy had been more of a father to them than their dad had. "I wish Granddaddy was here too. Of course, if Granddaddy was here, I sure wouldn't be marrying today. Manipulating old coot."

Linda nodded. "He always was a manipulator, but he loved

this ranch. And you four boys."

"Then why did he leave the ranch in equal measures to us and cousin Travis? Why not just to the four of us?"

Linda shrugged. "He probably felt it was only right to leave it to the five of you equally. Cousin Travis might not be your favorite person in the world, but he's your aunt's son. He has as much right to it as you four."

Karlan didn't argue. His cousin had been the worst as they were growing up, but he was married now, with two kids. That had mattered a great deal to Granddaddy. He couldn't help but wonder if he and his brothers had married, if the will would have been easier for them.

As they walked to the big house from Karlan's house, only about a quarter mile away, Karlan picked all the wildflowers he could find. If she didn't like some, then she didn't have to use them. His house was just far enough from hers for privacy, but still close enough they could go home for dinner every night if they felt like it. The men's homes were all about the same distance from their mother's home and from each others, their houses making a half circle behind her house on the ranch.

Instead of going to find her, he handed his mother the fistful of flowers he'd collected once they got to the big house, and she carried them back to her bedroom. "Hope, Karlan picked some flowers for you. We can make them into a bouquet."

Hope stared at the flowers in Linda's hand, her face lighting up with pleasure. "That's so sweet!" Karlan hadn't seemed like the romantic type to her earlier, but maybe she'd read him wrong.

Linda smiled, handing the flowers to Joy, who held her hand out for them. Faith was still fussing with Hope's make-up. "You look beautiful," Linda said softly, her eyes filling with tears. "I can't believe one of my boys is really getting married."

Hope smiled, hoping her nerves didn't show on her face. All at once, she wished the rest of her family was there with her, while being glad they weren't there. "Thank you for making it so easy to join your family."

"I've always wanted daughters. I'm excited to have one finally." Linda hurried to the mirror and brushed away the tiny bit of mascara that had run. "I never wear make-up, except for special occasions."

"You don't need it," Joy told her.

Linda laughed. "You haven't seen me without it yet. Wait until you do!"

The doorbell rang then. "Oh, that must be Brother Anthony and Lovanne. Hurry and get ready so you can join us." Linda rushed out of the room to go to the pastor.

Lachele walked over to Hope, taking both her hands in hers. "Are you nervous?"

Hope laughed. "I'm standing here praying for the earth to open up and swallow me. I would say I'm a little nervous."

Lachele laughed. "He's a good man. I hope you know I've investigated him. He's a good mayor, a good businessman, and he has an incredible reputation. I couldn't find a fault in his past. I think you're going to be happy with him."

Hope nodded. "He seems very sweet." She was thankful for

his agreement on waiting for sex. She was nervous about the wedding still, but it made it easier knowing he didn't expect that immediately.

Chastity rushed from the room without a word to anyone.

"She probably had to pee again," Faith said, rolling her eyes.

Hope laughed, feeling some of the tension ease out of her at the familiar complaint. "Why can't she just go when we're stopped somewhere?"

Lachele looked between the sisters. "Did Chastity have bladder issues on the drive here?"

"Chastity always has bladder issues," Joy said.

"Next time you go on a car trip with her, you should get her a box of Depends. You could totally bling them out so she'd like them better and actually wear them. No need to stop all the time!"

Hope stared at the woman for a moment, not sure if she was supposed to laugh or agree with her. Thankfully, Chastity burst back into the room. "I got you this for your wedding night!" Chastity announced, a grin on her face. She handed Hope a white box wrapped nicely with a lavender ribbon.

Hope looked at the box for a moment, afraid to open it. "Should I open it now? Or later?"

"Now! I want to see your face when you open it!"

Hope sighed. "I was afraid you were going to say that," she mumbled.

"What?" Chastity asked.

"Nothing." Hope took hold of one end of the ribbon and tugged on it, untying it. She then slid the box open, and stared down at a frilly piece of red see-through lingerie. She couldn't imagine ever wearing it. "Thank you, Chastity. It's lovely!"

"Look under it!" Chastity was practically bouncing up and down with her excitement.

Hope was more afraid than ever as she moved the frothy piece of fabric out of the way. Oh. Dear. God. A vibrator. One that looked like it was simulating an elephant penis. The thing was enormous!

"Just in case he's not good in the sack!" Chastity explained, her face lit up with excitement.

"I—appreciate it, Chastity. Thank you for thinking of me."

Chastity hugged Hope. "I love you so much. I hope you're happy with Karlan."

Hope smiled. "I'm sure I will be."

Lachele stepped forward. "Sorry to interrupt, but I think it's time to get out there. The pastor's here. The men are waiting. Let's get this show on the road, ladies."

Hope watched as her three sisters left the room to go out to join the men. There was no one to give her away, but that was okay. The wedding was small. She could walk herself down the aisle. How hard could it be?

She hurriedly closed the box and moved it to the floor outside of Linda's bedroom. She'd get it after the wedding and not feel like she needed to ask permission to go back into Linda's room. That would be perfect. Then she just had to find a place to dispose of the gift. Too bad Faith's kiln hadn't arrived yet.

She slowly walked down the hallway toward the living room,

where she could hear people. As soon as she saw Karlan, standing there in a formal suit, her heart started racing. He looked good as a cowboy, but he looked just as good in his formal attire. All she could think about was going to the man, grabbing him, and kissing him silly.

Of course, that led to thoughts about where kissing him silly could lead, and she started shaking. By the time she was at Karlan's side, she was shaking like a leaf, and having to force her breathing to stay calm. Why was this so hard for her?

Brother Anthony smiled at Hope. "Dearly beloved, we are gathered here today to join these two people, Karlan and—" He looked over at his wife. "Lovie? What's the bride's name again?"

"Oh, you should be able to remember that, dear! It's Hope! I hope you'll get it right!" Lovanne giggled behind a white handkerchief.

"That's right. Hope. We're gathered here to join Karlan and Hope in the state of holy matrimony. Of course, they'll still be in the state of Wyoming when they're in the state of holy matrimony. Why do they call matrimony a state? Do you know, Lovie?"

"No, but the bride is nervous, so you just keep going with the wedding, Tony!"

"Yes, dear." He faced the couple again. "Do you, Karlan, take this sweet woman to be your wife?"

It was obvious to Hope he'd forgotten her name again. Who was this man? She couldn't wait to go to a Sunday service if he was the one preaching. He was going to be a lot more entertaining than Pastor Rick back home. Pastor Rick talked about hellfire and damnation for sixty percent of his sermons. The other forty percent was spent picking apart the flaws of everyone in the congregation.

"I do." Karlan smiled at her as he said the words. He squeezed the hand he was holding as well. She wondered if he could tell how nervous she was and was trying to help.

"Do you, insert bride's name here, take Karlan to be your lawfully wedded husband?"

Karlan leaned toward the pastor. "Her name is Hope."

"That's what I said," Brother Anthony retorted.

"I do," Hope replied, biting her lip to stifle her laughter.

"I don't think you need to repeat anything after me, since you both said, 'I do.' So you're man and wife now. Kiss her, you fool!"

Karlan leaned down and brushed his lips across hers, keeping the kiss soft and gentle. He slipped his arm around her shoulders and turned toward their families gathered there. "We'll get rings later," he whispered.

Hope nodded, very much at ease after the wedding. Brother Anthony was a real gem.

The others crowded around them, hugging them both. Linda held Hope for a moment longer than the others. "I have a daughter!"

Hope laughed. "I hope I live up to your expectations."

"Of course you will!" Linda turned and hurried into the kitchen, pulling out two trays of finger foods. "I had a feeling at least one of the boys would marry today, so I made these last night."

Lachele grinned. "I knew it would be Karlan. He's not the patient sort, is he?"

"Not true!" Karlan protested. He looked at Hope. "Okay, so it's true. But I try."

Hope grinned at him, liking the look in his eyes. "I appreciate all efforts. Especially if they're geared toward being patient with me!"

She walked over and picked up a tiny sandwich from the platter on the counter, taking a bite. "This is good!"

Karlan watched her, and watched the way she interacted with her sisters and his mother, as well as Lachele. It seemed she didn't even notice his brothers. "You know, I should probably introduce you to my brothers, and it might be a good idea for me to meet your sisters," he said softly, his lips against her ear.

Hope felt a tingle rush through her body at his innocent gesture. "Sounds smart." She motioned for her sisters to come close. "This is Faith," she said. "This is Joy." Joy waved. "And that's Chastity." Hope said a silent prayer that Chastity would, just this once, keep her mouth shut.

Karlan smiled at all of them, before turning to his brothers. "That's Cooper and Kolby. The two of them are completely dedicated to the ranch. And that's Chris. He's a science teacher."

"Really? A science teacher?" Hope was surprised, but she wasn't sure why. All four brothers looked like they belonged on a ranch. "Do you help out on the ranch as well?"

Chris nodded. "Of course. I only work during the school

year. I'm an itinerant teacher, going from homeschooled family to homeschooled family, teaching the higher level sciences."

"I've never heard of that as an occupation. Very interesting."

"Chris kind of invented his own job," Karlan said, obviously dismissing his brother. "What did you do back home? Wow, I don't even know where back home was. Mom just told me in her text earlier that you'd traveled thirteen hundred miles, but she didn't say from which direction!"

Hope laughed, taking his hand and leading him to the sofa, where she sat close beside him. "Back home is Kentucky. We were in a small town, near Paducah. My sisters and I weren't allowed to work. We occupied our time with crafts."

"Not allowed to work?" The words came from Linda. "Why weren't you allowed to work?"

Hope smiled sardonically. "Our parents believed that a single female's job is to find a man to marry. They didn't think any girls should work on starting a career when they'd just be required to quit as soon as children were born."

Karlan frowned. "Why would you be required to quit when you had children?"

"Because a woman's place is in the kitchen, of course." Hope shook her head. "Faith makes dolls, and I've always sewn clothes for them. I also volunteer a lot of time with children. I teach Sunday school at our church. I work with kids after school. I volunteer in the local schools, doing whatever anyone needs. I do what it takes to keep busy."

"How did your parents expect you to occupy your time?"

"Searching for a husband, of course. What else would we do?"

He blinked a couple of times. "Are you serious? Is anyone really that backward in today's world?"

Hope sighed. "Only my parents. Don't worry. I don't expect to be a wastrel."

He shook his head. "I don't care if you work. We don't really need the money, and it's always nice to have laundry done and dinner ready and whatever else women do when they're home all day. But…if you want to work, you can work. I have no desire to control you that way."

She smiled sweetly. "I may just take you up on that."

The front door banged open, slamming against the wall. Karlan immediately stood when he saw his cousin, Travis, standing there. "What do you want?"

Travis's eyes focused on Karlan. "I see you decided to follow Granddaddy's will to the letter. Married already?"

"You're not going to get this ranch." The way the will was worded, those who were married would inherit the ranch. Travis was married. "I'm married now too."

"You know as well as I do, I don't want your stupid ranch. In fact, what I really want is for the ranch to be sold. I want my share."

"We're not selling the ranch!" Karlan yelled, before he realized he'd even raised his voice. "How can you want us to sell off the ranch that's been in our family since the 1880s? Don't you want your children to understand their heritage?"

"Why would I care? I want the cash. Sell off a fifth of it."

Karlan shook his head. "We're not selling off one square inch of dirt. This whole place belongs to Culpeppers. After a hundred and thirty years, it's going to keep belonging to Culpeppers."

"I've contacted a lawyer, you know." Travis studied his nails as he spoke. "I'm taking you four boys to court. You've got six months to buy me out, or I'm going to insist on a sell-out." He waved before turning and leaving.

Kolby took off toward the front door. Karlan ran and grabbed his brother's arm. "Don't give him the pleasure!"

"I'm going to kick his citified butt. That man doesn't know what a real man does with his time. No, he's not getting our ranch."

Karlan sighed. "He's not getting the ranch. I don't know how we're going to come up with that kind of cash in six months, but he's not getting our ranch." He rubbed the back of his neck. They could easily come up with about a fifth of the money necessary. He didn't want to mortgage the ranch, but he would if he had to. Travis was not getting a single acre.

Kolby closed his eyes and nodded. "He's not getting it. You're right. Kicking his butt would do no good."

"No, it wouldn't. We're just going to have to figure out how to make a little more money."

Hope looked at Faith. Faith nodded. Chastity and Joy walked over to Hope, each putting a hand on her shoulder. They may not have been allowed to use them for making money, but all the sisters had skills. Their men were about to wonder what hit them.

They were going to help save the ranch.

Out of the corner of her eye, Hope saw Linda watching them. She'd help them. Hope was sure of it. Monday, the four of them would sit down and have a meeting. In the meantime, it would be Hope's job to crunch some numbers.

Chapter Four

Much later that evening, Karlan drove Hope and her SUV over to his house. The men had unpacked the vehicle, putting Joy, Faith, and Chastity's things into the house first. Hope had left her things in the vehicle, ready to get them into her permanent home.

When he stopped in front of his house, he led her to the door, surprising her when he swung her up in is arms and carried her over the threshold. Hope let out a gasp of surprise, not having expected that. He set her down in the living room, leaning down to kiss her softly. "Welcome home, wife."

Hope smiled, leaning into him. "I think I'm going to like it here."

He smiled, tapping her nose with his index finger. "You explore while I bring your stuff in."

Hope wandered through the house. It wasn't big, but it wasn't tiny either. There were three bedrooms and two bathrooms. She went into his room first, eyeing the big bed for a moment. Soon she'd be sleeping there with her husband. Shaking her head, she walked away. She wasn't going to start obsessing about sex like Chastity.

She went into his bathroom, looking around. There were two sinks, and a separate shower and bathtub. The bathtub was a huge one, and she looked forward to soaking in it.

Next she went into the kitchen. It was large with an island in the middle and well-laid out. She'd be able to cook there comfortably.

The living area looked like it was designed for comfort. There was a cozy sectional sofa and a large screen TV. From there, she went down the hall to the other two bedrooms. There was a bathroom in between.

One room had a full-sized bed and a small dresser. The other had a desk. Hope decided her sewing machine could go in there. She'd start making the outfits for Faith's babies just as soon as she could. They had to help out the men. And she had some thoughts about how she could make money on her own as well. Yes, there would be no problem paying off that awful cousin.

Karlan carried her suitcases and boxes into her room, making several trips. "How did you get all this stuff here?" he asked.

She shrugged. "We shipped a lot ahead to your mom's house, but we also strapped the suitcases on top of the car and put the boxes in the back. We probably should have strapped Chastity to the top, but it didn't seem like an option at the time."

He chuckled, setting down the last of her boxes into her room. "That's done. Anything more coming?"

She bit her lip. "Well, our younger sisters are shipping the rest of the stuff."

"Younger sisters? There are more of you?"

Hope nodded. "Grace and Honor are twins. Didn't I tell you that? I thought I had. They're still at home in Kentucky. I wish you had two more brothers for them. I hate that they're still stuck at home with Mom and Dad."

"It really doesn't sound like a place I'd want to be. We'll figure something out for them." He patted her arm. "Do you need help unpacking?" She was still in her bridal gown, and he knew she needed to change out of it soon.

She shook her head. "No, I'll go ahead and change. Are you hungry? We had snacks at your mom's but I can cook something."

He nodded. "A little. Are you a good cook?"

She laughed. "I have a degree in Homemaking. Did you know that's even something you can get a degree in today? Well, you can!"

"Why did you get a degree in Homemaking? It was your choice, wasn't it?"

"It's all our parents would allow. I managed to minor in Accounting, but my parents didn't know that until after I'd graduated."

"I'm glad you're here and not under their rule any longer." He pulled her to him, kissing her forehead. "I'm ready to have a wife."

She smiled. "Let's go see how well-stocked your kitchen is. I may have to buy groceries before I can cook."

He shrugged. "I have some basics, but really not much."

She spent a minute in the kitchen taking inventory. "Okay, I can do bacon and eggs with toast. Or French toast. An omelet. Not much else. I'll hit the grocery store Monday. Are we going to church tomorrow?" She was actually excited at the idea. She'd never wanted to go back home, because the pastor had been so negative in his sermons. Brother Anthony would be a treat to listen to, though.

He shook his head. "Not this week. We'll go next. Brother Anthony made sure I knew if we went to church tomorrow, he'd have to assume I wasn't man enough to keep you occupied. Of course, he called you my new wife instead of Hope. I don't think he knows your name yet."

Hope giggled. "Probably not. At least he didn't call me 'insert bride's name' again."

"He loves his congregation!"

"He'd have to! No one would have him otherwise."

Karlan leaned against the counter, watching her as she cooked. "What did you decide to make?"

"I'm making omelets. If you want something else, now is the time to say something."

"Omelets sound good." He watched as she efficiently cracked eggs into a bowl and used a fork to mix them. Her movements were practiced. "You seem to have done this before."

She rolled her eyes. "Oh, once or twice. Mom made sure we were all ready to be wives. That means knowing how to cook the perfect breakfast for our husbands."

"You've led an interesting life."

"No, I haven't. That's the problem!" She deftly folded the omelet, standing over it, watching it cook.

Five minutes later, they sat down, and he took a bite of his omelet. "You're good at this cooking thing. Forget getting a job. Just keep cooking for me."

Hope dropped her fork. "You said I could do whatever I wanted!"

"I'm kidding! It was my way of complimenting you on your cooking." He was shocked to see that her face had turned white. "I'm not going to try to control you. I promise."

Hope nodded, picking her fork back up. He'd shocked her with his words. "I hope not. That's the one thing I can't stand for."

He reached out and took her hand in his. "You won't be asked to. I promise. You can cook for me, you can go get a job in town, or you can start your own business. Whatever you want to do, you can do with my full support."

"Thank you."

Karlan sighed. "That was really in poor taste, and I'm sorry. I thought you'd know I was joking."

"When you think about where I've come from, why would you think I would understand that?"

"You're right. I shouldn't have said it."

They finished the rest of their meal in silence, and when they were finished, Hope immediately cleared the table and loaded the dishwasher before joining him in the living room. She sat beside him on the couch, curling her feet under her.

Karlan's arm immediately went around her shoulders and he pulled her to him, his brain working at how he could talk her into his bed that night. He'd promised to not push anything, so if she said no, he'd have to stop. But oh, how he didn't want her to say no!

He found a repeat of *Friends* and put it on the TV, sure that she had seen it a million times like the rest of the country.

Hope found herself glued to the television immediately, her eyes wide. "What show is this?" She'd never been allowed to watch anything where there had been allusions to the fact sex existed, and here were characters openly talking about erogenous zones.

"You've never seen *Friends*?" He stared at her in disbelief. "Where did you say you're from?"

She shrugged. "My parents were very strict with us. When we went to college, we weren't allowed to live in the dorms. They knew what time we were out of classes and expected us home exactly an hour later. They bought us one vehicle to share between us, putting it in my name. All of us were in the same classes. My first kiss was this afternoon on your mother's porch swing."

He gaped at her. "Your first kiss ever? Not just your first kiss with me?" How was that even possible?

"Yes, my first ever. Joy has never been kissed either, and I don't think Faith has."

"What about Chastity? Shouldn't she be the one who's never been kissed?"

Hope smiled ruefully. "She's always talked about rising above her name. She never met a man she didn't want to kiss."

"How did she manage to kiss men when the rest of you couldn't find a way?"

"The rest of us didn't find the idea of saving ourselves for marriage repulsive. Only Chastity."

"So she's been with men?" Karlan asked.

Hope shook her head. "Oh, never. She didn't have that much freedom. The rest of us didn't find ways to kiss the boys under the bleachers at school though. Chastity did. I spent most of my formative years coming up with excuses for why Chastity was missing. I didn't have time to pursue a relationship of my own!"

"No wonder you want some time." He shook his head. "I don't know if I'm pleased or disappointed."

"Why would you be disappointed? You knew I wanted time to get used to the idea of being married."

"I was hoping I could talk you into changing your mind."

She laughed. "Not a chance. To be honest with you, the idea of sex with someone I love is kind of scary. The idea of sex with a man I met this afternoon is absolutely petrifying. No, we won't be having sex this week. Probably not next week either."

He sighed. "All right. Do I get to try to persuade you though? I mean, I think I should at least have that opportunity."

She blushed, but nodded. "You absolutely have that right."

He leaned down and kissed her softly. "Then I will take that right. I want our marriage to be a real one as soon as possible."

"I'm not going to make you wait years or anything. Just let me get used to kissing you and touching you before we go beyond that."

"I can deal with that idea." He grabbed her around the waist and pulled her onto his lap, kissing her passionately. "This is how I mean to persuade you, just so you know."

She laughed. "I reckoned as much." She felt tingles rush up

her spine. Her belly tightened as he kissed her. "You make my insides feel all funny."

"Glad to hear it," he whispered against her lips. He desperately wanted to touch her breast, but he forced his hand to stay at her waist. She didn't need to be rushed into anything. He could just sit there and kiss her for hours.

Hope pulled away from him mid-kiss to stifle a yawn. Three days on the road were finally catching up with her. "I'm sorry!" She didn't want him to think she found his kisses boring, because really, the opposite was true.

"I understand. You drove a long way to get here." He kissed her one last time. "Why don't you head off to your bed. Mornings start very early on a ranch."

"How early?" she asked. She'd always been an early riser, up at seven even when she didn't have to be.

"I'm usually up by five," he said. "I doubt I will be tomorrow, because no one is going to expect me to work." He frowned for a moment. "Would you promise me something?"

"What's that?"

"Don't tell anyone we're waiting to have sex. I don't want my brothers to know about that yet."

Hope nodded. "I would never embarrass you that way. I wouldn't trust my sisters not to say anything, so it'll be between us." She pressed a kiss against his lips before standing. "Besides, I don't think it will last very long anyway."

"I sure hope not." Karlan got to his feet. "It seems strange to say good night to my bride in the living room."

She smiled. "It seems strange to your bride as well. Give me a little time." She pressed her lips against his and wandered away down the hall toward the bathroom. She needed to shower and brush her teeth. Then she had to put her things away. No matter how tired she was, she'd been taught not to leave her things out that way, so she would put them up before bed. She could sleep in a little tomorrow. No one would expect a new bride to be up and around so early.

*****

It was after midnight when Hope fell into bed, so she slept much later than she'd planned. When she finally got up at eight-thirty, she found that Karlan had left her a note explaining where he was.

Hope,

I didn't want to wake you, so I made myself cereal. I'm out working on fences with my brothers, but I'll be back at noon for lunch, and we'll spend the afternoon together. Get some rest.

I'm going to tell my brothers that I wore you out so much, I'm letting you spend the morning resting. Keep the story going for me, would you?

Your husband,

Karlan

She smiled at the note, taking it into her room and putting it in the drawer of her nightstand. As soon as she opened the drawer, she frowned. She hadn't known where else to put the lingerie and elephant-sized vibrator Chastity had gotten her. She didn't want anyone to see it, so she was afraid to even throw the thing away.

She put the note on top of it and shut the drawer. She'd think about it another time. She wanted to get to the big house before lunch time, so she could talk to her sisters about the ranch's financial situation. She wanted to be able to help, and she knew that with the combined powers of her and her sisters, they could do a lot.

She hurried to dress and brush her teeth, and then walked over to Linda's house. She didn't know if the others had gone to church, but she had a feeling they were all too tired after the long drive they'd made.

She knocked on the door, and Linda opened it, a smile lighting up her face. "Good morning, Hope."

"Good morning. Are my sisters up yet?"

"We're just sitting down to breakfast. Have you eaten?"

Hope shook her head. "Actually I haven't. I slept in, and Karlan was gone before I woke. He made himself cereal."

"I'm not surprised. That car trip took a lot out of you girls. Sit down and eat with us." Linda waved her hand at the table where her three sisters and Lachele were sitting, eating breakfast.

Hope walked over and took an unoccupied chair. There was a veritable feast on the table including scrambled eggs, sausage, bacon, hash browns, biscuits, and gravy. She fixed her plate while she thought about how to approach the subject of finances with her sisters.

"I've been thinking," she said, and her three sisters gave her their full attention. She'd always been a leader for the others, especially where financial matters were concerned. The others had a mental block where math was concerned, barely making it through their required college courses, and she handled their money for the most part.

"I'm willing to use my full power to help," Faith said softly, knowing what her sister was about to say. They all fought sometimes, but they were quadruplets. They had a very special bond.

Hope nodded. "I knew you'd say that, but I think we'll need more." She looked at the other two.

Joy nodded. "My yarn, canvas, and patterns are here. I'm opening up an Etsy shop tonight, and I'll start an eBay account as well. I know plastic canvas Barbie Doll furniture and buildings may sound strange, but I'm good. People are going to buy my stuff."

Hope put her hand over Joy's squeezing her sister's fingers. She turned her attention to Chastity.

Chastity smiled. "I'm going to knit socks. Special socks." She leaned closer to Hope, who was sitting beside her. "I'm going to find other stuff to make too."

Hope closed her eyes before nodding. She just hoped Chastity didn't get *too* creative with whatever she made. "Can you share Joy's Etsy account and eBay?"

"Absolutely!" Chastity grinned. "I can't wait to get started!"

"I'm going to start a daycare in our house. I'm sure there are plenty of local families who need childcare," Hope announced.

Linda looked around at the sisters. "Are you doing this to

help with finances?"

"Of course," Hope answered quickly. "We'll do anything we can to help, and these are the things we're good at."

"Use my house for the childcare then. I'll help with the children. I'll help with any of the projects. I prefer to paint, but I'm very crafty."

Hope nodded, a smile covering her face. "Sounds good to me. I think if the parents know that you'll be here, it'll be easier for them to sign their kids up for Culpepper Care."

"You have my full backing with any of the projects!" Linda said, obviously excited that the girls were planning to help. "Just tell me what I need to do."

Hope smiled. "We'll do it together. Everything starts tomorrow."

Chapter Five

Hope and her sisters did the breakfast dishes, as much to have time to talk privately as anything else. "Faith, you should really tell Linda about your babies. She's going to be supportive. You know that."

Faith shuddered. "You know, I want to. I'm so used to hiding it that I feel like I should at least for a little while longer. I'll tell her soon. I promise."

Hope sighed. "I think we need to just come clean about everything with them. This family is so different than Mom and Dad. Linda seems to actually care what we have to say and realizes we have personalities. She's not grouping us all together as 'the quads.' I want to sit and talk to her and spill my guts."

"Feel free. Just don't spill your guts on my secret. That's my place."

"She knows you make dolls. She knows you're going to sell them to help pay off the family's debt. Why not just tell her everything?" Hope really didn't understand her sister's worries about being honest.

"I'm not doing it." Faith bent over to keep loading the dishwasher. "Not yet, anyway."

Hope sighed. "Whatever."

When they finished, the sisters all went into the living room to join Linda and Lachele. "I think you owe me a story," Hope said. "I want to know about how Wiggieville got its name!"

Linda smiled. "Well, I know the story, but I don't know how much of it is historically accurate. Back in the 1860s or 1870s, no one is sure which, there was a new settlement in Texas, between modern day Dalton and Stephenville. A woman lived there with her children, and when her oldest son married, his wife had a little boy. Now that little boy, for reasons known only to him, called his grandmother 'Wiggie,' and he told stories about that grandmother as if she was some sort of superhero. He thought she could do absolutely anything, and she was the most wonderful woman alive. When it came time for the town to be named, the boy kept begging for the town to be called Wiggieville. No one had a better suggestion, and everyone had started calling the woman Wiggie, so they all agreed. The town has had the same name ever since."

Hope grinned. "I like that story."

"I still think I want my grandma name to be Wiggie, if that's all right with you four girls. Of course, if the grandkids start calling me something else, well, that's fine too. They can call me pretty much anything they want."

Chastity grinned at Hope. "Just think, you could be pregnant right now! I hope your wedding night was everything *I* dreamed it could be!"

Hope elbowed Chastity, refusing to discuss it. "I think that's a lovely idea. If the kids want to call you Wiggie, that's great. If they want to call you something else, I think they should."

"I agree. It'll be like I'm getting a surprise that way. Who could complain about getting a surprise from her grandbabies?"

Hope glanced at the clock and saw that it was after eleven. "Oops. I'm supposed to make lunch for Karlan and have it ready at noon. He doesn't even have any food!"

Linda laughed. "The boys always come here when they get hungry." She walked to the fridge. "Karlan loves grilled cheese sandwiches made with pimento cheese." She gave Hope everything she'd need to make the sandwiches. "Does he have butter? Or should I send some?"

Hope laughed. "No, he has butter. Maybe some chips? I'll replace whatever when I go to the store tomorrow."

"Oh, no need. And you two come here for supper tonight. I'm sure he doesn't have what you'd need to make a real meal."

"We had omelets for dinner last night, so we'll need to take you up on that."

Linda packed everything into a paper sack and handed it to Hope. "There. I don't need anything back, but I might send you with a short list for the grocery store tomorrow."

"I wouldn't mind a bit. I'll need to stop by before I go anyway. I need to know where to apply for a daycare license and all that good stuff. We're going to make sure Travis doesn't force the men to sell."

Linda shook her head. "I hope we can keep from selling off even a portion of the ranch. The boys are very proud of this place."

Hope hugged Linda tightly. "We'll be back for dinner, or if

not, we'll text and let you know."

"Sounds good."

Linda watched Hope leave with a smile on her face before turning back to the others.

*****

At exactly noon, Hope put four grilled cheese sandwiches on a plate and shut off the stove. She carried the plate to the table and looked at the Cheetos she'd poured into a bowl. It certainly wasn't the type of meal she'd ever expected to cook for her husband, but she could make do with whatever was on hand.

The door opened and Karlan walked in, his shirt unbuttoned, and sweat dripping down his chest. Hope couldn't tear her eyes away. She'd never thought she would be the type to fall for a muscle-bound cowboy, but one look at her new husband, and she knew she'd been wrong. Maybe it was just this particular muscle-bound cowboy, but she found she wanted to go over and lick one of the rivulets of sweat off his chest.

As soon as she thought about licking him, a blush slowly creeped across her face until she felt like it was burning. "What do you want to drink with lunch?" she asked, looking down to hide her embarrassment.

Karlan grinned. "Now what is that blush about, wife?" he asked, striding across the entryway and dining room to where she stood.

"I don't know what you mean," she fibbed.

He put a finger under her chin and lifted her face up to his. She was a tall woman, the tallest of all her sisters at five-nine, but he was so much bigger. Why he had to be six-three or so. "What are you embarrassed about?"

She shook her head, knowing she couldn't tell him what she'd been thinking. "Nothing."

He leaned down and pressed his lips against hers. She immediately wrapped her arms around him, her hands going under his open shirt to stroke his bare back. "Tell me."

"What do you want to drink with your lunch?" she asked, as soon as he lifted his mouth.

"You're really not going to tell me?"

"Nope. We're married, not joined at the brain."

He sighed. "Sweet tea is fine if there's some made."

She nodded. "I made some while I was making sandwiches. There's really nothing here for me to cook for supper, so your mom invited us to eat there."

He shrugged. "That's fine, I guess. I would rather spend the time alone, but I will get hungry."

"We could walk over and just stay for the meal and leave."

"That works."

She poured them each a glass of tea, before taking a chair. He sat in the same place he had the night before. "You should have woken me up this morning. I would have made breakfast for you."

He shook his head. "I peeked in at you and saw everything you did last night before bed. There was no way I was going to wake you."

"You could have. My mom has always gotten up and cooked a good meal for our family in the mornings. That's what I was expecting to do." She felt bad that she'd slept late. "Instead I went over to your mom's and had breakfast there."

"I'm glad you're getting along well with Mom. She has some friends in town, but we're far enough out that she doesn't make it in often." Karlan took a bite of his sandwich. "Your grilled cheese is just as good as Mom's."

"She gave me the ingredients and told me how you like them. I'm going to have to do some grocery shopping tomorrow if you want me to keep feeding you."

He frowned. "I'm a little worried about money. The whole thing with Travis is scary. I don't want to sell off part of the ranch. I don't want to take out a mortgage on it, and we don't have a lot of ready cash."

She reached over and took his hand. "My sisters and I discussed it this morning. We're all going to do everything we can to help."

He raised an eyebrow. She had never worked a day in her life. How did she think she could help? "How?"

"Well, I'm going to start a daycare at your mom's. We're calling it Culpepper Care. Faith is going to sell the dolls she makes." She hated that she couldn't just come out and tell him that her sister had been selling them for years and making a tidy profit off them too! "Joy is going to make plastic canvas Barbie stuff and sell it. Chastity is going to knit socks and other stuff." "And you really think your crafts will make a difference for us?"

Hope shrugged. "Depends on how hard we work them. We can certainly make enough to help. If we all cut corners at the same time, maybe we can manage without a mortgage or anything."

"I appreciate it," Karlan told her, looking like he was dubious. Really, what did she know about making money when she'd never even worked?

After the lunch dishes were done, Karlan took her hand and pulled her into his room. "This is my first Sunday afternoon off in forever. I'm going to use it wisely."

"Oh, really? How are you going to do that?" Hope was surprised he'd brought her into his room.

"I'm taking a nap with my new wife."

Hope felt her heart jump into her throat. "I'm not ready for that."

"I didn't say I was making love to you. I said I'm taking a nap with you." He pushed his shirt off his shoulders and kicked off his boots. Pulling a pair of clean shorts out of a drawer, he tossed her a T-shirt. "I'll go in the bathroom and put shorts on. I can sleep in those, and you sleep in the shirt."

He went into the bathroom and Hope sprang into action, quickly stripping and putting the shirt on, carefully keeping her back to the bathroom door so he wouldn't see her if he came out unexpectedly. She debated keeping her bra on, but it was too uncomfortable to sleep in. So what if he saw the outline of her nipples? He was her husband!

She was under the covers when he came out of the bathroom, and he smiled when he saw the stack of neatly folded clothes on the dresser. He slid into bed beside her, moving to the middle and gathering her into his arms.

"I really am planning to sleep. I just want to do it while holding my new wife. You know, like people sleep holding teddy bears."

She laughed. "I've never been compared to a child's stuffed toy, but okay. I guess that works."

He kissed her briefly, before resting his head on the pillow. She put her head on his shoulder. "This feels nice," he said. He liked holding her. He'd like it if she'd let him whip out his ding-a-ling a lot more, but for now, he'd be content to hold her.

Hope smiled. "I feel like I'm doing something wrong just being in your bed. I think I may have some—hang-ups about sex."

He grinned. "I bet I can help you work through them. Want to start now? Or later?"

She laughed. "Later is probably better for me. I really am tired." She never took naps, because she was always busy, but napping in his arms sounded blissful. "G'night, Karlan."

He kissed the tip of her nose. "G'night, Hope."

*****

Hope woke to find herself on her side facing away from Karlan, her bottom nestled against his groin. There was definitely something going on there. She started to ease away from him, when his arms tightened around her, and he pulled her right back. "Where do you think you're going?" he asked, his lips against her ear, causing shivers to run down her spine.

"I thought you were still asleep," she said. "I was going to get up and go do something useful." She had planned to cut out some of the little Halloween outfits. She'd already bought the fabric. She'd always found that if she cut out all of one type of outfit at once, things went quicker for her.

He brushed her hair out of the way, before kissing the side of her neck, biting it gently. "You're useful right where you are, darlin'." His voice was filled with Texas for the first time since she'd met him. She shivered.

"Not as useful as I could be out there," she said.

"You know we have to make a baby, right?" he asked softly. He didn't know what all she'd been told about the provisions of the will, but he did want her to understand.

"Now?" she asked, her voice barely squeaking out.

Karlan's deep laugh filled the room. "No, not right this second. Unless you want to, of course."

Hope sighed. "When then?"

"Soon. One of the provisions of my grandfather's will was that all four of us had to get married for any of us to inherit. And then one of us has to have a baby on the way within a year. If none of us has a baby on the way, then we forfeit the ranch and it goes to Travis."

She shuddered at the thought. "Why Travis?"

"He's our cousin. He's been married for five years. Has two of the worst behaved children I've ever seen. The will says he gets a tenth of the profits of the ranch forever, unless he chooses to help work it, in which case he gets a fifth."

"Will he help work it?" she asked.

"Not for all the gold in Fort Knox. The man is the laziest

human being I've ever met. He's afraid of horses." His voice was filled with disgust as he said the words.

Hope frowned. "I don't know how to ride. I've never been on a horse."

"That's different! You weren't on a ranch for an entire month every summer growing up. You didn't have a grandfather who was dying to teach you how to ride."

"No, I didn't. I would like to learn."

"I'll teach you at the same time I teach our first child. So, you wanna make a baby now?"

She blushed at his words. Was he going to ask her that every time they talked? "Not yet. Soon."

He sighed dramatically. "I was sure it wouldn't hurt to ask, but you know what? It did. It always hurts to be rejected."

She giggled, rolling over so she faced him. She felt his erection against her leg as she rolled, knowing he must be uncomfortable, but he still treated her with respect. She could get used to being married to a man like him.

"How can I make it up to you?"

He raised an eyebrow and a slow grin spread across his face. "I have several ideas!"

"I was thinking I could make your favorite dinner tomorrow night. Not whatever it is you're thinking."

"Well, dagnabbit. I wasn't thinking about food at all."

"I'm sure you weren't!"

He took one finger and traced it down the side of her face, along her collarbone, and down her shirt. He moved it to her nipple, and gently stroked her through the thin white fabric. "You're beautiful, wife."

Hope blushed. "Want to know what I was thinking earlier? When I blushed?"

"Yes. Are you ready to tell me now?"

"I was thinking you looked really sexy with your shirt open and sweat dripping. I kind of wanted to lick your chest."

Karlan grinned, a slow sexy smile that tied her stomach in knots. "Any time, sugar."

Hope leaned forward and licked his chest, right above his nipple. "Salty."

"I didn't think you'd really do it!"

She laughed. "I maybe be inexperienced, but I'm very curious. I like how you taste."

He groaned. "Don't tell me that! I'm already so turned-on I feel like I'm going to break."

"Oh?" She didn't know what had gotten into her, but she leaned forward and sucked at his neck for a moment before pulling away. "I think I'm going to like this marriage thing."

"So am I. Just as soon as you let me strip you and introduce you to Charlie."

"Charlie?"

"My ding-a-ling, of course. He's ready to meet you now, if you're interested!"

Hope pushed away from him. "I think I'm going to go get a shower and work for a little while. I promised Faith I'd make some clothes for her baby dolls."

He watched as she rolled to a sitting position, grabbed her clothes, and rushed from the room. His shirt hit her mid-thigh, and he wanted to chase after her and throw her onto the nearest bed. Or floor. Or table. Or counter. He didn't care where it happened. Just so it happened. What was it about that sweet little thing that kept his body in knots and his ding-a-ling hard enough to chop down a tree? She was pretty special all right.

Chapter Six

While Karlan answered emails and made some phone calls, taking care of his mayoral duties, Hope cut out clothes for the babies at the kitchen table. She'd purchased the soft orange fabric in bulk, and she was certain she could make the fabric, meant for twenty outfits, stretch to twenty-two. The more she could stretch it, the more profit they'd show. She wouldn't have even tried two days ago, because they made more than they needed, but now, she'd do anything she had to do.

One of the things she'd learned in her homemaking classes was how to be frugal. She was about to put that into play. She would use every coupon she could get her hands on, and she would make sure they squeezed every dime until Roosevelt cried.

She'd put on some yoga pants and a comfortable top to work in, knowing it would be a long day if she tried to work in jeans. She hated jeans anyway. They just weren't comfortable. Her mother would have preferred she never wore pants, but she and her sisters had refused on that one point. They'd be comfortable, no matter what their mother said.

After a particularly long and angry sounding phone call, Karlan looked at what she was doing. "What exactly are you making?"

Hope grinned. "Twenty-two pumpkin outfits for baby dolls."

"Twenty-two? Why pumpkin outfits?"

"Well, I think if we sell holiday outfits in sets for Faith's baby dolls, we could make a huge profit off of them. A lot of women want to use the dolls in their decorations, but they don't have the time to sew the clothes. It would be cheaper than buying the outfits separately somewhere else, and they'd be getting one for each season."

"Are you sure the dolls will sell?" he asked. "You really think women are going to buy the things?"

Hope laughed. "Wait until you see them. You'll understand. Yes, they'll sell. And these outfits will do really well for us. I can sew them while the kids nap."

"You know, Mom paints, but she's really crafty in other ways too. If you need some help with anything, just put her on it. Mom can do anything."

"I'll keep that in mind." Hope was thrilled he wasn't laughing at her. Yes, it must seem like a strange idea to him, but he was being encouraging. That's what she needed. She set her scissors on the table and walked over to him, plopping herself down on his lap. "Thanks for not laughing at me."

"Why would I laugh at you?"

"My parents always laughed at us when we talked about our skills. They didn't see them as marketable."

"I'm willing to give anything a shot." Karlan wished he could erase all of the mental damage their parents had done. He couldn't help but wonder if his brothers knew how their parents had treated them.

She kissed him quickly before jumping back up. "I want to get these all cut out before supper. What time does your mom eat?"

"We should probably get there before five," he answered.

Glancing at the clock, Hope realized she only had another hour. She still had to do the green stems for the hats as well. She picked up the pace.

Karlan held Hope's hand as they walked over to the big house, going right in the back door. All of Karlan's brothers were there, dressed in jeans and clean button-down shirts. They had all obviously showered and shaved after work and were paired off with her sisters.

Hope squeezed Karlan's hand before walking toward the kitchen. "Do you need any help, Linda?"

Linda shook her head. "No. Lachele's been helping me. She has to be at the airport in a few hours, so this is her last meal with us."

"I'm sorry. I know you've enjoyed having her here." Hope was sorry she hadn't had more time with the matchmaker herself. She was a good woman, and just strange enough to keep life interesting.

"I'm sorry, too. I'm sure she'll be back though. I told her she could set up office right in Culpepper, and she'd have no problem staying busy."

Hope grinned. "I don't think she'd be as busy as she is in Manhattan, though. And she probably wants to go home to her husband, Sam."

"And Margarita! Don't forget about my dog, Margarita!" Lachele called as she carried her suitcases into the dining room, setting them against one wall. "I'll be leaving right after supper."

Linda looked at Hope. "Oh, everyone's here. Hope, would you stir the sauce for a minute! I want to go get something I made for everyone."

Hope walked around the counter that divided the dining room from the kitchen, stirring the spaghetti sauce. Karlan stood watching her with a grin. "What?"

Karlan shrugged. "Isn't a man allowed to enjoy looking at his wife?"

Hope grinned, blushing a little. "I guess it's all right."

Linda came back into the room with five gift bags, setting one on the counter beside the stove, one at Lachele's feet, and giving one to each of Hope's sisters. "I made all of you gifts, but I wanted to give them to you all at once. I'd planned to do it after lunch yesterday, but we were suddenly getting ready for a wedding." She took the spoon from Hope. "Not that I'm complaining."

"Should we open them now?" Hope asked.

"Yes! I love watching people open gifts!"

Hope opened hers, and it was a lap quilt. She pulled it out of the bag, and rubbed it against her face. "Oh, it's so soft! Thank you, Linda." She reached over and hugged her mother-in-law.

"You're so welcome! I'm glad you like it."

"I adore it. It will be really nice on cold winter nights."

Hope watched as each of her sisters opened a similar quilt, each with different colors. Chastity's quilt had little pickles all over it. Hope covered her mouth with her hand.

"You gave me pickles! How did you know I love cucumbers?" Chastity asked with a giggle.

Linda shook her head. "There's just something about you, Chastity. It's pretty obvious where your mind is."

Faith held a quilt with tiny little dolls on it. She hugged it to her. "It was like you knew us before you ever met us."

Lachele and Linda exchanged a glance, and Hope understood then. Lachele had told her the personalities of the girls coming to marry her boys. How clever!

Joy's quilt had little puppies on it, and Hope smiled. Joy had always loved animals, but their parents had said pets were too messy, so they weren't allowed to have them. Joy would be thrilled to have a puppy of her own.

Hope looked at her quilt more closely, and she saw a smaller quilt pattern, obviously showing her love of sewing. "You must have worked really hard to get these done in time."

Linda shrugged. "It's not a big deal once you get started."

Hope shook her head. "I disagree. I've done some quilting, and I know how big of a deal it is."

Linda put the food on the table while the girls compared quilts with each other. Hope was surprised her sisters weren't helping more. She cornered Faith and asked her about it.

"We're helping with most meals. Linda specifically told us that when the men are around she doesn't want us to help. She wants us to concentrate on getting to know them."

"I see. That makes sense then." Hope was satisfied with that answer.

After supper, they all said a tearful goodbye to Dr. Lachele. Hope was surprised how close she felt to the woman on such a short acquaintance. "Come back and see us soon," she said.

"Find a man in the area who needs a wife, and I'll do my best," Dr. Lachele said with a grin as she hugged Hope tight.

"I'll do my best. You have to find a way to interview Grace and Honor, as well. They need to come out here and join us."

Lachele nodded. "I'll try."

After she was gone, Hope looked at Karlan, expecting him to be ready to leave. He seemed to be deep in discussion with his brother, Chris, though, so she turned her attention to her sisters. "I'm going to drive into town in the morning. I need to see about getting a license for my daycare, and I need to get some groceries. Does anyone want to go with me?"

"Oh, yes. Linda told me there's a doll store in Culpepper. I'd love to look at it, and maybe see if I ever build up an inventory of babies if we can sell them in the store," Faith said.

"Oh, good idea." Hope looked at Chastity. "How about you?"

"I'll stay here with Linda." Chastity smiled at the older woman, obviously already having bonded with her a bit.

"Joy?" Hope asked.

"Yeah, I'll come. I want to see what kind of shops are local to us. I don't want to have to drive super far for supplies or have to buy everything online." Joy frowned. "I have a lot of stuff to get started with, but it seems like you always have one or two things you forget to buy.

"Okay, three for Culpepper in the morning." Hope turned to Linda. "Do you need me to pick anything up for you?"

Linda pulled a piece of paper off the fridge that had been fastened by a magnet. "I made a list."

Hope took the list and read over it, before tucking it into her pocket. "I can do that. I'm going to act like we're going to have a full house for our daycare Tuesday through Friday of this week. I know it won't fill up that fast, but I'm going to have the stuff for meals and snacks, just in case."

"I think that's smart. If there are no kids this week, at least you'll have it for next week. We'll freeze anything perishable, just in case."

"We'll go to town in the morning, but in the afternoon, I'd like to sit down and plan activities. I will want there to be a well-scheduled day." Hope looked at Linda. "I saw an old swing set out behind the house. Do you think it's safe for children?"

"Definitely. Especially with supervision, which we'll be sure they always have."

Karlan walked over to Hope, taking her hand. "You ready to go home?"

Hope nodded. "I'll be back tomorrow morning. I think we'll leave for town around nine? Does that work?"

Joy and Faith nodded, before returning to their men. Hope hugged Linda. "See you tomorrow."

As they walked home, Karlan asked what her plans were for the next day. "I need to go into town to see about getting a daycare license and do some grocery shopping. Faith and Joy want to check out Culpepper as well. See if there are any shops that will help us. How far is it to Culpepper anyway?"

"It'll take you about twenty minutes to get there. It's a small town, and you might get some looks. There's a lot to do for the for childcare license, but I'll pull some strings and get you pushed through faster. Why be mayor if I can't help out my wife with little things like that?"

"Why would I get looks?"

Karlan laughed. "It's a small town made up of mostly men. You're pretty girls no one knows. Trust me. You'll get looks."

Hope blushed. "It's a good thing I'm already married."

He squeezed her hand. "Yes, it is." He frowned as he thought of something. "We'd talked about getting rings after the wedding. I'm not sure about that now. We need to sink every dime into savings, so we can buy Travis out."

"I understand. The ranch is a lot more important than a ring."

He let out a sigh of relief. "I'm glad you understand."

"Just so I get a ring someday."

"Absolutely!"

When they got back to the house, she piled up her fabric pieces she'd left out and put them into the craft room. It wasn't late enough to sleep, but Karlan seemed very distracted to her, so she wanted to stay out of his way. When his phone rang, she got out the red and white fabrics and started cutting out the Santa outfits for Christmas for the babies. Why not? He was too busy for her anyway.

He made phone calls on and off all night, and finally put his phone down at nine. "I have an emergency city council meeting tomorrow night." He rubbed the back of his neck. "What are you making now?"

She grinned. "These are little Santa outfits for the babies."

He shrugged. She certainly knew how to keep busy and stay out of trouble. Those were good qualities in a wife. "I'm going to have to go into town right after work tomorrow. You can either spend the evening with your sisters and Mom and probably my brothers as well, or you can stay here. Up to you."

Hope smiled. "You know, I like the idea of having some time to myself. I haven't really been alone in my life. I've always shared a bedroom with a sister. I've always had someone with me, because our parents figured if we traveled in pairs, we wouldn't get into trouble. A night alone sounds good."

Karlan made a face. "Married for less than two days, and my wife is already glad to get rid of me."

Hope laughed. "Not glad to get rid of you at all. But happy to savor the time I've been given to be alone."

He grabbed her and pulled her to him, kissing her madly. "Okay, you go off to your lonely bed, and I'll go to mine. You sure you don't want to play a game of slap and tickle?"

"Slap and tickle?"

"Do you prefer getting frisky? Bumping uglies? Aggressive cuddling? Assault with a friendly weapon? Bedroom rodeo?

Boinking? The pickle tickle?"

She just stared at him for a moment. "Are you finished?"

He shrugged. "For now. I'll save some for later."

She stood on tiptoe and brushed her lips against his. "Good night, Karlan."

As she wandered off to her solitary bedroom, he watched her with a grin. She was something, that wife of his. He didn't necessarily believe she and her sisters could raise any money, but he sure did think a lot of her for trying. She was a good woman.

*****

Hope woke up to her alarm at five, rubbing her eyes. Wandering into the kitchen, she put bacon on to fry as she whipped up the egg and milk mixture she needed to coat the bread for French toast.

By the time Karlan made it into the kitchen, she had breakfast on the table and was pouring them both a cup of coffee. He didn't say a word, but simply picked up his coffee and took a big sip.

"Do you want milk as well?"

He nodded, obviously still tired. "That'd be great."

"What do you do for lunch while you're working?" she asked.

He shrugged. "I usually go to Mom's. She'll fix me a sandwich."

"Oh, all right. I'll probably still be in town at lunchtime today, and since I'll be working there, that sounds like it's something that should continue."

"Sounds good to me." He sat down at the table, liberally buttering and adding syrup to his French toast. He took a bite of the bacon and smiled at her. "Perfectly crisp. Is there anything you can't do?"

"Ride a horse. Someday, I'll learn to do that too, though."

He smiled, grabbing her hand and pressing it to his lips. "Yes, you will."

After she kissed him goodbye, he walked toward the stable, which was situated between the houses. She immediately made the beds and cleaned the kitchen. Then she started on her sewing. She sat in the room she'd dubbed the craft room with the tiny little pumpkin outfit pieces.

By the time she needed to leave for the big house, Hope had finished three of the tiny little outfits. She wanted to giggle at how cute they'd turned out. She carried them with her to show her sisters, hoping that Faith had one of the babies with her to try them on.

She went in the back door, understanding Linda didn't want her to knock. She saw Faith sitting at the table knitting away at something with Chastity. "Why are you knitting?" Hope asked with surprise. They all knew how to do each other's crafts, of course, but Faith's time was much better spent with her doll sculpting. None of the others were at her level of expertise.

"My clay hasn't arrived yet," Faith said with a frown. "And even if it had, my kiln won't be here for a while yet."

"That's true," Hope said. "You have to see what I did this morning." She pulled the tiny outfits from behind her back and held them out for Faith to see.

"Oh, those are darling! I didn't quite understand what you

meant until right this second." Faith jumped up from her chair. "I have Sara with me. Let me try it on her." She rushed off down the hall, while Linda came out of the kitchen to see what Hope held.

"Oh, those are cute! Are they for the dolls Faith makes?"

"Yes, what do you think?" Hope wasn't sure how much Linda knew about Faith's business, so she kept the whole tone casual.

"They're so cute! I want a doll, and I want one of those cute outfits. I love decorating for Halloween."

Hope smiled as Faith ran back into the room with Sara. She put the life-like doll on the table and stripped the clothes off.

Linda stared at the doll for a moment. "That looks so real! It's amazing! Where do you get the heads?"

"I sculpt them," Faith said with a smile. She held her hand out for the outfit, and Hope handed it to her. A minute later, she held the baby up with the orange pumpkin outfit on.

The little orange and green stem hat made Hope giggle. "That's exactly how I pictured it!"

"Oh, it's wonderful, Hope! How long did it take you to make these?"

"I cut them out yesterday, and that took about three hours, but I managed to cut twenty-two out of fabric that was supposed to be for twenty. And then I've been sewing since six. So about six hours, so far, but I'm getting faster. I think I'll be able to sew the others in under thirty minutes each, now that they're all cut out."

"So you could conceivably do a whole set every day, even with the daycare."

"I absolutely think I could."

Faith nodded, obviously excited. "That's awesome! I think we can charge even more than I was thinking for them."

Joy walked in, looking at the baby. "Oh, that outfit is adorable. You did great, Hope!"

Hope grinned. "Thanks!" She looked at Linda. "Did you think of anything else you need?"

Linda thought for a minute before shaking her head. "No. I think I'm all set."

"All right. We'll be back in a few hours. We'll probably eat lunch in town."

Linda nodded. "Have a good time."

As they were walking toward the door, Hope hissed at Chastity, "Behave yourself!"

"I always do!" Chastity said with a sweet smile.

Hope frowned, but walked back toward the house she shared with Karlan, her sisters at her sides. "If I'd been thinking, I'd have driven over this morning. Sorry you have to walk."

"Oh, no big deal," Faith said. "It's good for us."

"How's married life?" Joy asked, a twinkle in her eye. "I've been afraid to ask with Chastity there, because she'd want to ask about the size of his pickle."

Hope shook her head. "Karlan's a good man. I'm glad we're married." She didn't add anything, not wanting to accidentally give something away. She'd promised Karlan she wouldn't tell her sisters about their arrangement, and she'd never been able to keep a secret from them.

The town was just as small as the one they'd grown up in, but the doll store there was unique. Faith talked to the owner about her business, showing her the website on her phone. The owner agreed that if she ever caught up with orders and had an inventory, she'd be happy to sell them.

There was a small yarn store in town which thrilled Joy to no end. "This will be perfect for getting the little things I need. I mean, they don't have the canvas, but I'll buy that in bulk anyway."

Next they stopped at City Hall to apply for a childcare license. The process was quite easy, and the girl they spoke to seemed excited. "My mom is sick of keeping my son while I work. Do you take two year olds?"

"We'll take any age up until they start school."

"Oh, that's awesome! I'm Tiffany, and I'll be bringing Sebastian out tomorrow. Mom is going to be so happy!" Tiffany couldn't have been much older than twenty, and she bounced as she spoke to them.

"I'll look forward to that. What time will you bring him?" Hope asked.

"Seven-thirty or so. I need to be here at eight."

"That's perfect. You know where the ranch is?"

Tiffany laughed. "Oh, every girl for miles around knows where the Culpepper Ranch is. Those men are too handsome to go unnoticed."

Hope frowned at that. She didn't like the idea of all the girls in town checking out her husband. "I'm married to Karlan."

"Congratulations. That one is a real catch." Tiffany winked

at her, making Hope feel better about the whole thing.

After they left there, it was off to the grocery store. "We have our first kid. I'd better buy food for twelve. I don't think we can handle more than that."

"Sounds good to me," Joy said. She didn't care much about the childcare, because she had her own work to do, but she'd help out whenever she needed to. They all would. Hope hadn't asked, but the answer was unspoken. Sisters help sisters.

Despite their financial troubles, Hope knew she was where she needed to be. She was finally happy. If only she could get over her fear of making love with her husband.

Chapter Seven

After putting away the groceries, Hope, Joy, and Faith all returned to the big house to talk strategy. Hope carried her iPad with her, knowing it would be the easiest way for her to take notes on what they discussed.

Joy spread her arms wide as they walked. “I love Wyoming! This air is so fresh and the people are so nice! And there’s a sexy cowboy kissing me every evening.”

“Oh? Kissing? Kolby?” Hope asked. She felt like she’d been a bad sister since they’d arrived in Culpepper, not paying as much attention to her sisters’ lives as she should.

“Yes, Kolby. He’s incredible.”

“You’re not mad at me for snatching Karlan up before anyone else got a shot at him?” Hope asked.

Joy and Faith both laughed. “Not at all!” Faith said. “I wouldn’t have Karlan on a bet! He seems so boring.”

Hope grinned. “Really? Karlan?” His kisses set her on fire, but her sisters thought he was boring? What was wrong with them? Or was something wrong with her?

“Yes!” Joy said. “I’ve spent time with all three of the other brothers, but Kolby is the man for me. I wouldn’t want Karlan.”

Hope linked her arm with Joy’s. “I’m so glad. Sisters before misters!"

Joy laughed. "We've always said that, but it never mattered before now. Of course, we all knew Chastity was lying when she said it."

"God love Chastity," Faith said. "I love her, but she's nuts. She says she and Chris haven't done the deed yet, but they sneak off when they think no one is looking."

"I'm not going to think about it!" Hope declared. "I'm going to set up a business plan for Culpepper Care today." She paused for a moment before looking at Faith. "Do you think you could up your production at all? I know you don't have your stuff yet, but when it gets here? Your business is established, so I think you'll have a better chance to make more than the rest of us."

Faith nodded. "As soon as my clay and kiln are here, I'll be working like a madwoman. We're all as determined to make the finances work out as you are, Hope."

"Good. If you can make even twenty-five percent more, that would be awesome." Hope had no idea how much they needed to earn, so she wanted to maximize every minute of time to make as much as they could. She'd always been the numbers girl, so it was up to her to make it happen.

"I think I can do that. I'll do my best. I wonder if Chastity could make little socks." Faith looked contemplative at the idea.

"I bet we could talk Linda into making baby quilts for them if we explained why!" Joy suggested.

"We could even just tell her that we're hoping to sell them. She knows we're doing an Etsy store and eBay. I bet she'd make doll quilts for that." Hope didn't want to turn Faith off of any idea that might help them make money. As long as she didn't have to tell her secret, Hope was sure Faith would be agreeable.

"We could do that," Faith said. "Are you going to make notes about everything and tell us how much to charge to make it worth our while?"

"Is the Pope Catholic?" Hope asked.

They walked in the back door of the big house, finding Linda and Chastity at the table together. Linda was cutting out quilt blocks, and Chastity's knitting needles were flying as she worked on a pair of socks.

"What are you making, Linda?" Hope asked, putting her iPad down on the other end of the table from where Linda was set up with a cutting mat and a rotary cutter.

"I thought I'd try my hand at making a doll quilt. If we make them an add-on for your dolls, I think we could make some money from them." Linda looked at Faith. "Do you think that's a good idea?"

"I think it's brilliant! The more we can add on for the dolls, the more money we'll make."

"Oh, good!" Linda said with a smile. "I was afraid you'd think I was being presumptuous."

Hope shook her head. "We're all doing everything we can to make money to help out. I appreciate you thinking of it and being willing to work with us."

Faith sat down at the table. "I loved the doll shop in town. They said that they would take any extra dolls we end up with."

"That's wonderful! Do you have any idea what you'll sell them for?"

Faith shrugged. "Hope is in charge of all that. She's our money person."

Hope turned her iPad on and looked at the others expectantly. "We'll have at least one child starting tomorrow. He's two and his name is Sebastian."

"Oh, sure. Tiffany Snow's little boy. Her mother is so sick of having to run after a toddler all day." Linda shook her head. "I'd love to be privileged enough to run after my grandbaby."

The phone rang then, startling Hope. "You have a home phone? I didn't think they even existed anymore!"

Linda laughed, walking over to answer the phone. "Hello? Oh, sure. Yes, we're planning on starting tomorrow. Stacy and Bob? Yes, we'll be ready for them. Thanks!" She looked at Hope. "Stacy is four and Bob is two. We're going to start out with three, I guess."

The phone rang pretty consistently after that as word spread through the small town that someone was opening a childcare. By the end of the afternoon, they had eleven children signed up to come the following day. Hope did some quick math, working out the profit for each child.

"I'll need some help with meals and watching the kids. Is everyone on board with this?" Hope looked at Faith. "You'll be the last I ask for help once your supplies are in, but I will still need to ask some."

"Of course. We're all in this together."

Hope smiled, continuing with the menu planning she'd started before the phone calls. "Chastity, would you prefer to watch the kids in the morning while I cook lunch? Or do you want to cook lunch while I watch the midgets?"

"I'll watch the kids with Linda. They're more fun than standing around in the kitchen surrounded by pots and pans."

"That works for me. We'll all have craft time in the evenings and during nap time. Most of us should be able to get some craft time in during the day as well." Hope turned to Linda. "I'll do crockpot meals for us every day for supper, unless I can cook whatever we're having quickly. Could you plan to do breakfast for the children? Sounds like the earliest will be here at seven."

Linda nodded. "I'll take care of breakfast every morning. All of the parents know me, so it will be easy for them to drop off to me. What time are you planning on getting here?"

"Probably six-thirty or so. That'll give us time to get everything we need to have together for the day. Most of the kids are either in the two-year-old or four-year-old age range. If you take the two-year-olds, I'll take the four-year-olds. I can do a lesson plan that will teach them their numbers, letters, and colors. All of that important stuff."

"Sure. That sounds great. I'll go get some of the boys' toys out of the attic, and we can get them cleaned up and ready for a new generation of children." Linda hurried off, heading toward the garage.

Faith looked at Hope. "Do you really think we can make enough?"

Hope nodded, her eyes lit up. "I really do. I think the men will be very pleasantly surprised with the kind of money we'll be bringing in. They don't have a lot of faith in us yet. Let's show them what we can do."

"Why do people always underestimate us?" Joy asked.

Hope shrugged and looked at the clock. "I need to get home if I'm going to make dinner for my husband. I'm going to try and make a few of the Santa outfits tonight. I'd like to have one of each made up, so that we can put them on the website to let people know that they're for sale. By the weekend, we should be able to add a page for them."

"That's a great idea. Hopefully, I'll have my kiln within a week. I can't wait to be able to work on my 'little hobby' full-time. Mom's going to be so mad when she hears what we're doing." Faith didn't look at all upset by that idea.

Hope waited until Linda got back. "Since I need to leave, can you guys make sure that that stuff gets cleaned and sanitized before the kids get here tomorrow?"

Chastity nodded. "I'll take that over."

Hope smiled at her sister. "Thank you. I really appreciate it." With a wave, she hurried out the door to walk home. She could cook a real meal for her husband that evening, and she was thrilled.

While dinner was in the oven, she quickly sewed three of the Santa outfits. She kept watching the clock, and finally at six-fifteen, she remembered that Karlan had said he had a city council meeting and would eat in town. She frowned, removing the food from the oven. He would have a good meal to eat for lunch the next day if he wanted it.

She ate her solitary meal, excited to have the evening alone, even while she was disappointed that she wouldn't get to spend time with Karlan. After putting his meal into the refrigerator and washing the dishes, she went to work on the St. Patrick's Day outfit.

By the time Karlan walked in the door, she had the first three little green shamrock outfits sewn as well as little Easter outfits. Only two more to go. She knew she wanted to do a onesie for the Fourth of July, but it was the last one that was befuddling her. She wanted six outfits, and she only had five. She'd have to think on the last one.

"Are you hungry?" she asked, running to the door to kiss Karlan. "How was your meeting?"

He rubbed the back of his neck, the gesture she was learning he made whenever he was stressed. "It was long. No, I'm not hungry."

"Okay. Anything I can help with?"

He shook his head. "I need a shower and my bed." Walking down the hall toward his room, he called over his shoulder, "G'night!"

Hope was surprised. It was the first time she'd spoken to him when he hadn't tried to get her into bed. Was he mad at her?

Karlan stripped and stood under the shower spray. He couldn't listen to one more word from anyone. It had been an awful meeting, with bickering from both sides of the traffic light fiasco. Half the council members were sure a traffic light would be the ruination of their calm, old-fashioned town. The other half were just as convinced that if they didn't get the traffic light, plagues would rain down from heavens over them. Why couldn't people just get along?

He was paid a very small salary as mayor, but he'd decided that he and Hope needed to find a way to live on that little bit until they found a way to pay Travis what he wanted. He still didn't know why Travis thought it was all right to bankrupt the thing that had made their granddaddy happy, but if that's what he had in mind, they weren't going to give him the satisfaction. Thankfully his house and truck were paid for, so they should be able to make it with their expenses. He wished he could give Hope the world, but that wasn't going to happen. Not yet anyway.

Hope stood in the living room for a few minutes after Karlan shut his bedroom door wondering what she'd done to offend him. Was he angry that she wasn't willing to have sex yet, even though he'd agreed before they married? If he was, he was just going to have to live with it, because she wasn't ready for that!

She went back into the craft room and started up the sewing machine, cranking out two more outfits before bed. The man could be infuriating; there was no doubt about that. She just wished she was allowed to talk to her sisters about it. She knew it would make her feel better.

*****

Karlan was still distant during breakfast the next morning. After tossing and turning all night, Hope needed to find out what his problem was. Whatever she'd done to annoy him, she wanted out in the open so they could deal with it.

"What did I do?" she asked as he was taking a bite of his eggs.

"What do you mean?"

"I want to know why you're mad at me. I didn't do anything wrong that I know of, so just spit it out so we can deal with it." Hope had never been one to pussyfoot around any negative situation.

He shook his head. "Why do you think you did something wrong?"

"You were gone all evening, and then when you came home, you went right to bed. You only kissed me once, and that's because I kind of forced it on you. If that doesn't mean something's wrong, I don't know what does."

Karlan rubbed the back of his neck, and Hope's eyes narrowed. "The city council meeting last night was awful. The council members are divided over something stupid, and it ended up as a shouting match. I was so annoyed when I got home, that I thought it would be better if I didn't inflict my bad mood on you."

She frowned. "Really? That's all it was?"

"Yeah. I'm sorry I made you think otherwise. We've been trying to decide if we're going to put in a traffic light on Main Street. You'd think it would be an easy decision, but with the way the council is reacting, our decision is going to cause Armageddon to come early if we choose the wrong thing." He made a face. "We've been fighting this same subject at every meeting for six months. One of the members called an emergency meeting last night, and I thought we'd get it resolved once and for all. Nope. Everyone is still mad at each other."

Hope shook her head. "That sounds ridiculous."

"It is." He stood up. "I have to go. We're starting to brand the cattle this morning, and it's a long process." He grabbed her hand and pulled her to her feet and against him. "You could tempt me to stay if you wanted to play hide the cannoli." He kissed her sweetly.

She wrapped her arms around his neck and kissed him back. "Hide the cannoli, huh?"

"Oh, yeah. I've been dying to play it with you."

"As tempting as your offer is, I have eleven kids who will be arriving at your mother's house in the next couple of hours. I think your mom and my sisters would appreciate it if I came and showed them the schedule I've worked out for Culpepper Care."

"Fine. We'll do the tube-snake boogie later." He grabbed his hat from the counter, shoved it on his head and left, closing the door behind him.

"The tube-snake boogie? Where does he get these?" She hurried through her morning chores, started supper in the crock pot, and hurried over to the big house. She couldn't get her silly husband out of her mind, though, and she knew she was walking around with a goofy grin on her face.

As soon as Chastity saw her, she giggled. "Someone must have spent some time doing the horizontal polka with her husband this morning."

Hope blushed and sat down at the table, pulling out the schedules she'd printed off for everyone the night before. "I made a schedule of our events of the day for everyone. Faith, I'm assuming you're working with us until your stuff arrives."

At Faith's nod, she continued. "I've got you helping out with outside time and helping me with numbers and letters for the older kids. If you can take over during those times, I can get some sewing done."

She'd finally decided to do a dress outfit as the last thing for the babies. The girls would get a little pink dress and the boys would get a pair of blue shorts with suspenders and a white shirt. They'd be cute, and she had the fabric she needed already. She was always buying more fabric than she needed. It was an obsession!

When the kids started coming in, Hope was surprised. Fifteen children showed up, four more than she'd planned for. Thankfully she'd brought extra snacks, so they'd be able to accommodate the bigger number. Each parent was asked to fill out a form explaining all of the children's allergies, special dietary needs, and preferences.

Linda had brought down several books for the children, and she even had a small slide that could go into the living room. There were many balls and stick horses. The children would not lack for things to do.

Hope divided them into groups, taking the four year olds and sitting them down for a talk about the rules that needed to be followed. She could already see that a little girl named Anna would be the smartest one in the group, as well as the one who would make sure everyone else followed the rules. A little boy named Roy was going to be the rule-breaker, tugging on Anna's pigtail during the talk about rules.

The day zipped by, even with the chaos that filled the air. Karlan stopped in for lunch. He had a way with the children that thrilled Hope, making her know he would be a good father. When his short break was up, he kissed her softly and hurried off, telling her he might be home late.

The last of the children left after six, and Hope sank into a chair, staring straight ahead for a minute. Her sisters and Linda all followed suit. "That was exhausting."

Linda nodded. "But fun! I can't wait until we have that many little ones running around all the time."

Joy looked at Linda, her face serious. "You don't want grandkids, do you, Linda?"

"Oh, no. No more than six hundred or so." Linda rubbed her hands over her face, obviously exhausted. "It's going to get easier once we're used to them, right?"

"Definitely," Hope told her. "Every day will get easier."

Linda got up and went to the kitchen, digging through the cabinets for something quick to cook. "I usually have this all planned out early in the day. Man, this is one of those days when I think the kitchen should be removed and someone should just put in a drive-thru window for deliveries."

Faith nodded. "That sounds good to me right about now."

Only Chastity was unaffected, but she'd spent the majority of the day knitting. She'd take breaks to come out and talk to the children, but like the others, she was on a mission to make as much money as possible. She knew she'd have her turn with the children once Faith's supplies arrived.

Hope got to her feet. "I've got to get home. I want to be there before Karlan is."

Linda smiled. "You know he'll understand if you're not."

Hope nodded. "I know he will. I just feel like I should be there first." With a wave, she hurried out the door. Karlan didn't have a meeting that night, so they would have the evening together. She was starting to feel like she knew him well enough to make love, but she wasn't going to tell him that yet.

When she got there, she hurried to set the table and put dinner on. She didn't have to wait long for him. He arrived ten minutes after she did, looking dead on his feet. "Long day?" she asked.

He nodded. "Very long day. Do I have time to shower before supper?"

Hope nodded. "Sure. That'll give me time to make some biscuits to go with the stew."

Karlan came back out twenty minutes later, looking refreshed. "How did the first day with the kids go?"

"Oh, really well. They're all angels."

He snorted. "I saw Roy Pettigrew put a frog down Anna Smith's shirt. He's an angel?"

"Well, he might be the exception to the rule, but he was sweet and well-behaved as could be while he was napping."

"I'm sure. That's probably the only time that boy is well-behaved. I saw him push a little boy down because he was blocking the water fountain at church one Sunday morning."

"Oh, I don't believe that!" Hope said with a grin. "The biscuits aren't quite ready, so start with the salad." She put the salad in front of him, a bottle of ranch dressing beside it. She knew he liked ranch, because it was the one of the few things that had been in his refrigerator when she'd arrived.

He started getting calls again right after supper, and spent the whole evening discussing city business. Hope did the dishes and then cut out more of the clothes for the dolls. She'd planned to take the evening off to spend with her husband, but if he was too busy, she'd certainly make the most of her free time.

When he finally put his phone down after the last call, he sighed. "Bedtime for me. Another tough day tomorrow." He kissed her briefly. "I'm going to bed." He was already in bed before she realized he had once again failed to ask her to make love with him. Was he losing interest in her already?

She cleaned up her mess and carefully put the pieces in a bag. She would work during the kids' nap time. Chastity and Joy had agreed to take over during nap time because their crafts were quiet while Hope's was loud.

Hope yawned as she headed into bed. It was going to be a long week.

Chapter Eight

That first day set a pattern for the week. The newlyweds woke early, went their separate ways, saw each other for a few minutes for lunch, ate supper together, and then Karlan spent the evenings on the phone while Hope worked on sewing.

On Friday night, she expected to have his full attention for a change, because she knew that she wouldn't be working the next day, but Karlan was again on the phone all night. When he finished his last call, she walked to him and sat on his lap, kissing his cheek. "What are we going to do tomorrow?"

He raised an eyebrow at her. "I'm going to have to work like I always do on Saturdays. I figured you'd spend the day with Mom and your sisters doing all your crafty stuff."

She frowned. She'd made good money that week with the number of children they'd ended up with, and she already had a waiting list for Culpepper Care. Of course, there was always more work to be done. "That's fine. I have lots of work I can do. I should probably spend a couple of hours cleaning the house as well."

Karlan looked around him, trying to see something that needed to be cleaned. The woman kept everything neat as a pin. "I guess."

She shrugged. “I’ll spend the morning with your mom and my sisters, and I’ll come back here to work after that.” She stood up, certain he wasn’t interested in spending time with her. Was he regretting he hadn’t married one of her sisters?

Karlan watched her, knowing he’d done something wrong, but not sure what. She didn’t want him to let Travis force them to sell the ranch, did she? “G’night, Hope.”

“Good night.”

Hope slipped off to her room, trying not to let him see the tears. She’d messed up their marriage by not being willing to consummate immediately. That had to be the problem.

She climbed into bed, worried about her marriage. What if they could never recover from her mistakes? Would he even be interested if she were to walk into his room and climb into bed with him?

She sighed. Faith was getting married tomorrow evening. She had to keep smiling for her sisters.

*****

After the wedding, Hope and Karlan walked home hand-in-hand. She rested her head against his shoulder. “It’s so beautiful out here at night,” she said. “I don’t miss Kentucky at all, and I was sure I would.”

“I’m glad you don’t. I don’t know how I’d react if my wife just wanted to run off back to her parents.”

Hope sighed. No matter how bad life got, she knew she’d never want to go back to her parents. “No, I like the freedom I have here. I’m working harder than I’ve ever worked, but I have so much more freedom. I love working with the children, and your mother is just darling. She's so helpful with both the kids and the quilts she's making for the dolls."

"You all seem to revolve your lives around those silly dolls."

"They're not silly. Trust me. You're going to be thankful for those dolls soon."

Karlan shrugged. "I'm not so sure about that. I guess if they make you and your sisters happy, that's a good thing, though."

"Are you working tomorrow?" she asked.

"Yeah, we have to work on the fences still." He sighed. "I hope Faith and Cooper have an easier time being together than we do. I swear, between my position as mayor, and your daycare and sewing, I feel like we have no time together at all."

"You could shut your phone off one evening per week," she suggested, holding her breath for his response. Would he agree?

"I would, if not for that stupid traffic light. We have to get that thing resolved as soon as we can."

Hope didn't say another word about it. When they walked into the house, she grabbed his tie and led him to the couch by it, curling up beside him and kissing him. She was ready to really be his wife, and ever since she'd made that decision, he was too busy to pay any attention to her.

Karlan was stunned when his timid little bride grabbed him and kissed him. He was all for it, though. She tasted sweeter than honey to him, and he loved touching her. He turned toward her on the couch, his hands going to her waist to pull her even closer to him.

Hope let out a small moan, her hands pushing his suit jacket off his shoulders before going to work on the knot of his tie. Ever since she'd seen him that day with no shirt on, she hadn't been able to stop thinking about his bare chest and wondering what the rest of him would look like with nothing covering him.

Karlan deepened the kiss, his hand going around to cup her breast through the silky fabric of the dress she wore.

The ringing of his phone startled him, and he sat up straight, pulling it out of his pocket. He looked at the number and cussed under his breath. "I don't want to take this, but I have to."

Hope just nodded, her eyes glazed. After a minute she got up and went to her bathroom, slipping into the shower. If he was going to spend all night on the phone, she was going to get some work done.

*****

Hope spent the next day at home, working on the books for Faith's business as well as adding up the profit Culpepper Care was already bringing in. Karlan had told her he wasn't going to draw a check from the ranch any longer, and they were going to have to live on his paycheck from the city, which was tiny.

When she was certain she'd done all the bookkeeping she could, she went out to her car and climbed behind the wheel. She needed to make a trip into town for groceries for the week. She had a better idea of what the children would eat now, so she could choose more wisely. She wanted to only serve healthy meals for the kids, but they all seemed to prefer pizza and chicken nuggets. Most of their parents said to feed them what they'd eat, so that's what she decided to do.

*****

Karlan went home in the middle of the morning, claiming that he had forgotten his work gloves. They were in his saddlebag, right where they belonged, but what he really wanted was to spend a few minutes with his sweet wife. Had she been trying to tell him she was ready to make love the night before? It had seemed like it, and then he'd blown it by taking that call.

He walked in and called her name. "Hope! Are you here?"

When she didn't answer, he went in search of her. She had done all the laundry and cleaned the bathrooms yesterday, as well as mopping all the surfaces. Now the whole house had a nice lemony scent. He first went into his office. He was shocked to see how well she'd settled in. There were little doll clothes everywhere, but no Hope.

He walked into her room, but again no Hope. He started to leave, but he noticed her nightstand drawer opened and something caught his eye. He walked over and rummaged through the drawer, his jaw dropping in surprise.

He picked up the vibrator from the drawer, turning it over in his hands. She wouldn't make love to him, but she was willing to use a toy like that on herself? Well, no wonder she didn't need him! He didn't know if he should be angry or disgusted.

He put the toy back in the drawer and slammed it closed. Wherever she was, she didn't need him obviously. Why would she?

*****

When Hope returned home from the store, she put the groceries away and sat down to write out menus for the week. She carefully wrote down what the children would eat for breakfast, snacks, and lunch every day, and then typed it into her laptop, printing it out.

When she finished that, she started dinner before going back into the craft room to get back to work on the doll clothes. Soon, she'd be done with this project, and she'd be able to go back to making the regular clothes and the bodies for the dolls. And she'd have twenty-two different sets of outfits ready to be purchased. They'd already sold four sets of clothes on the website since yesterday morning when she put them up. They were going to make a serious profit off this idea.

When Karlan came in at the end of the day, she kissed him like she always did, but she felt the need to step back quickly. If he was too busy for her, then she had to give the illusion she was too busy for him. She wasn't going to leave her heart unguarded that way.

As soon as he saw her, Karlan got annoyed. She was using sex toys and holding out on him. That was just rude as far as he was concerned.

While they ate, she asked questions about his day, but she seemed colder to him. Maybe he'd imagined her affection before. She probably didn't even know how to be affectionate.

After dinner, he started making phone calls, refusing to be sucked into her drama, while she did the dishes and went back to her craft room to work. When he got tired, he just went to bed without a word. Did he really owe her anything else?

Hope was sure her marriage would never work. Karlan was still keeping up appearances and pretending to have feelings for her, but he wasn't even kissing her anymore. Did he wish he'd married Chastity?

*****

Monday morning, Chastity seemed to be fixated on pregnancy. "Are you pregnant yet, Hope?" she asked.

Hope shook her head. "How am I supposed to know yet? You know it's not time for my cycle!" All of the Quinlan girls had been on the same cycle for as long as they could remember. Every month like clockwork, they'd all start craving chocolate three days before. When their father saw the chocolate start to disappear, he knew what it meant, and he usually tried to schedule a business trip for that week.

"But do you *think* you are?" Chastity persisted.

"I have no idea. Probably not. I don't think I'm fortunate enough to get pregnant the first month."

Joy smiled, getting into the conversation. "You know, I think we should take pregnancy tests together every month. There's one that's accurate three days before your cycle is expected. We could all take that test together at nap time."

Hope hated the idea, but she didn't want to be a party pooper. "Uh, sure. We can do that." So far only she and Faith were married, but that would change soon. Joy was getting married that evening. Hope didn't quite understand why her sister would want to marry on a weekday, and Joy hadn't explained it in a way that made sense to anyone.

"Mondays are kind of dreary days. I think a Monday wedding is a way to perk things up around here."

"Why are Mondays dreary?" Faith had asked.

"I don't know, but I intend to keep this one from suffering the usual Monday fate. I'm getting married."

No one had dared question her more. Joy got strange ideas into her head, and because they all loved her so much, they didn't dare argue with her. Joy was the sister who really did live up to her name, spreading joy to all those with whom she came into contact.

Faith shrugged. "I'm in for peeing on a stick together. Well, not together. I love you three, but I'm not peeing anywhere but a private room. Sorry."

Joy grinned. "No, peeing on a stick in private is the best way to do things, I'm sure."

"Are you excited about your wedding?" Hope asked. Joy was going to wear her wedding gown, because she hadn't taken the time to buy another.

"So excited! I can't wait to move in with Kolby!" Joy glanced over at Chastity. "Although, I'm a little jealous of Chastity getting Linda all to herself for a while."

Chastity made a face. "I know as well as you do that you're just saying that so I won't feel bad about being the last to marry. Well, I don't feel bad. I'm getting the best of the four guys, after all. I can't wait 'til I get him alone."

Hope smiled at her youngest sister. "I haven't spent much

time with Chris. Tell me about him."

Chastity smiled, staring off into space dreamily. "He's really smart. I love him for his mind."

Hope burst out laughing. "I can believe he's smart, but Chastity, you love him for his mind? Really? You care nothing about what's in his pants?"

"Oh, well, yeah. I'm sure I'm going to love little Chris as much as I love big Chris."

Linda walked into the room then, overhearing just the last part of the conversation. "Oh, you're thinking of names for the kids already? I love the idea of you naming my grandson after Chris. You don't even have to call him Christopher. You could call him Christian, and we'd all know he was named after Chris."

Chastity looked at Hope with wide eyes. Hope could see her sister wanted to correct Linda, but she was afraid to. Even Chastity knew not to talk about her future husband's male anatomy with his mother standing right there. "You tell me about Chris, Linda. I haven't really gotten to spend any time with him."

"Oh, Chris is definitely the smartest of the bunch. He does all the paperwork for the ranch, as well as the work he does teaching science. For a while I thought he was going to break tradition and become an astronaut, but instead he became a science teacher and helps his brothers on the weekend."

"Sounds like a nice man." Hope smiled at Chastity, hoping her sister didn't feel like she was getting the runt of the litter. She couldn't imagine being married to anyone but Karlan, even if things weren't perfect between them.

The doorbell rang then, and the kids started coming in. After that, it was full-scale chaos until naptime.

Hope went home to change after work, putting on the same dress she'd worn to Faith's wedding. They hadn't brought a lot of clothes with them, knowing Grace and Honor would ship anything they left behind.

She was already dressed for the wedding when Karlan walked into the house, hurrying to shower and change. She waited patiently, wondering what she could do to alleviate the tension between them.

When he came out of his bedroom, he was straightening his tie, and looking everywhere but at her. "Are you ready?"

"Yeah, I'm ready. Joy is really excited about marrying Kolby."

"Good. Kolby's excited too." He said nothing else, just opened the door for her so they could walk.

Hope waited for Karlan to take her hand, but he didn't until they were just outside the back door of his mother's house. "You haven't told anyone we're not sleeping together, have you?"

Hope shook her head. "I promised I wouldn't, so I won't. I'm always true to my word."

"Promises are interesting things, aren't they?"

Hope stopped walking and looked at him. "Have I done something to upset you?"

He laughed, and the sound was harsh. "Why would I be upset? I got just what I wanted, right?" He opened the back door, walking in before her.

Hope had no idea what was going through her husband's head, but she was tired of being treated like a leper. When they got home, she was going to confront him. There had to be a reason for his behavior. Whether it was logical or not remained to be seen.

Once the wedding was over, and they'd all had the supper Linda made, Karlan and Hope walked home together. "Brother Anthony was in fine form tonight," Hope said, wishing she could draw him out before they got home.

"He always is." Karlan stared straight ahead. If she wanted to spend her time with her vibrator, then she could, but she could have conversations with the stupid thing too.

When they got home, Karlan turned toward his room. Hope grabbed his arm. "We need to talk."

"About what?" he asked, his voice angry.

"About what's wrong. I don't know what you think I've done, but I've spent every ounce of energy I have taking care of your house, serving you meals, and trying to help the ranch out of the financial hole your cousin is determined to put it in. I want to understand what about that upsets you."

"None of that upsets me," he said calmly. "It's your little machine that upsets me."

"My machine?" Hope racked her brain, trying to think of what machine she had that would upset him. Her sewing machine? "If you're jealous of my machine, you have issues."

He stared at her in shock. She didn't even look embarrassed about having the thing! "I'm not jealous of it. I'm pissed that you'd choose it over me!"

"I'm yours anytime you want me. You're the one who's been shutting me out, not the other way around." She took a step closer to him. "Your phone calls are so much more interesting than talking to me or even kissing me. Obviously, you're the one choosing something over me."

He shook his head at her. "You really believe that, don't you?"

"I really do! When was the last time we had an actual conversation? Our marriage is never going to work if you don't talk to me."

He shrugged. "I signed papers saying I'd marry you within a month of your arrival and not try to separate for at least a year. That gives us eleven and a half months to go. I can make it. Can you?"

Hope took a step back, surprised at his words. "Are you giving up on our marriage already?" She couldn't believe it. She'd already started to fall—she shook her head, refusing to even finish the thought. No, she wasn't falling for him. He wasn't worth it.

She turned away from him and walked to her bedroom, closing the door softly behind her. She wanted to slam it, but she wouldn't give him the pleasure of knowing how much he'd upset her.

Undressing quickly, she put on her nightgown and got into bed. Staring at the wall in the dark, she tucked one arm under her. Why had this seemed like the ideal situation and the right thing to do?

Marrying Karlan Culpepper had to be the dumbest thing she'd ever done. At least her sisters were happy. Maybe knowing the situation had worked out well for them would help fill the emptiness she felt inside.

She wanted to scream and rage at herself. Why, just when she knew she'd lost him forever, did she realize she was in love with the jerk? Why couldn't her heart be logical?

She buried her face in the pillow and allowed the tears to fall. He wasn't worth them, but that didn't stop them from coming.

Chapter Nine

Two weeks later, nothing had changed between Hope and Karlan. They were barely roommates, not really speaking to one another unless absolutely necessary.

Hope was angry enough with him over his attitude about her sewing machine, she no longer had anything to say. Well, her brain didn't anyway. Her heart wanted her to throw herself at his feet and beg his forgiveness. Why couldn't he accept her as she was?

Their third Monday of marriage, she started dinner in the crock pot like she did most mornings, and fixed breakfast. "I have a council meeting tonight," he told her, the first words he'd spoken to her that day.

"All right." What did she care what he did?

After breakfast, she got up and did the dishes while he finished eating, bringing his bowl to her. He stopped at the door and turned to her as if to say something, but then he grabbed his hat and clapped it against his leg, leaving without another word.

Hope felt one lone tear slip down her cheek, and brushed it away angrily. He wanted to end their marriage as soon as he could. He didn't deserve her tears.

She got her craft bag ready, so she could work that day before leaving. Faith was back in full swing, and she only went to the big house if Hope called her begging for help. Joy and Chastity helped around their crafts, but mostly the work with the children was done by her and Linda.

Joy had made a huge castle for Barbie Dolls, and she was meticulously making the furniture for it. She planned to put it up on Etsy that evening.

Joy met her at the back door, her face glowing. "I got the tests at the store yesterday," she whispered.

"What tests?"

"The pregnancy tests! Today's the day we all take them together."

Hope's face fell. "Oh, yeah. Right. At lunch time?"

"I can't wait to see if some of us are pregnant. I know you'll probably go first, like you do with everything, but I hope I am too. I'm walking on air just thinking about it."

For once, Joy's overwhelming positivity was about to drive Hope crazy. "I hope you are too." Hope smiled at her sister, wishing she could hide her sense of doom. They'd always be sisters, of course, but when Karlan divorced her, they wouldn't have the same kind of bond. Would her sisters be torn between loyalty to her and loyalty to their husbands?

Hope was quiet through most of the morning, saying only what she needed to say to keep the children on task. Once the whole herd was down for their nap, she met her sisters in Linda's bathroom.

"This seems weird," Hope protested. "We're all just going to pee on the stick and line up the stupid tests?"

Joy nodded. "I'm so excited! I'll go first!"

Ten minutes later there were four pregnancy tests lined up on the counter, and Hope knew hers was negative. You had to actually have sex to be pregnant, after all.

All of Hope's dreams were right there in her negative pregnancy test. Her sisters would have babies and she wouldn't. She wanted to run from the house screaming, but that would be telling. No, she would pretend everything was fine until Karlan kicked her out. She'd promised, and she didn't break her promises.

When she got home that night, she decided she was taking the night off. She felt like the opposite of her name. She was hopeless, and it felt terrible.

She ate her dinner alone, sitting at the table in the dining room. She was happy that there would be babies and the terms of the will were fulfilled, but she was sad for herself. She didn't want to be alone.

She sat in front of the television and watched more of the show Karlan had shown her on one of her first nights there. Something called *Friends*. She laughed at the antics of the characters on the screen, thankful something could make her laugh with the way she was feeling.

When Karlan came in after nine, she turned to look at him. He looked dead on his feet, and her natural compassion took over. "Are you hungry? I made some Swiss steak."

He nodded. "I'm going to shower really quick, and then I'll

nuke some." He walked back to his room, and she jumped to her feet, microwaving the steak and the baked potato she'd made for him.

She had his meal on the table, along with a glass of sweet tea when he came out. Sitting beside him, she took his hand in hers. She smiled at him, when he looked at her with confusion. "Tell me about it. What happened?"

He sighed. "Would you believe two councilmen actually got into a fist fight because one of them said he'd leave town if the traffic light was put in?" He shook his head. "I ended the whole thing, though. I read last night in the town ordinances that I have veto power over any bill. I told them I didn't think the town was ready for a traffic light. So the debate is over. I'll veto it if it comes to me, which means there's no reason to continue."

"I bet you made some enemies."

He shrugged. "At this point, I don't even care. Their childish attitudes were taking up way too much of my time." His eyes met hers. "I do realize my ridiculous amount of time on the phone had a lot to do with us fighting."

Hope shook her head. "I understood."

"Can we start over?" he asked, his voice soft. "I don't want to spend the next year at odds with you. I want a real marriage."

Hope nodded. "That's what I want too. I tried to tell you that one night, but then the phone calls started."

Karlan brought the hand he still held to his lips. "Then let's have a real marriage."

Hope jumped up. "You finish eating. When you're done,

stick your plate in the dishwasher and run it. I'll be right back." She rushed from the room, knowing he would think she was making no sense, but she didn't care. All she could think about was the sexy little negligee Chastity bought her for her wedding night.

She showered quickly and shaved her legs. She refused to have hairy legs the first time she made love with her husband. What would he think?

She blew her hair dry before going into her room to put on the nightgown, wrinkling her nose when she saw the stupid vibrator. She had to get rid of the thing, but she didn't want anyone seeing it. Maybe she could sneak it into her car on Sunday when she did the grocery shopping and find a dumpster somewhere.

She pulled a robe on over her lingerie and then went out to join Karlan. He was just putting his plate and glass into the dishwasher. "Oh, you finished eating."

He nodded. "And I did the dishes." He eyed her in the robe, wondering what was underneath it. When he'd said he wanted to have a real marriage, he didn't think she'd jump up and get ready to go to bed with him. Not that he was complaining.

Karlan was still in the shorts and T-shirt he'd pulled on after his shower. She caught his hand and dragged him into his bedroom, planning on getting his clothes off him just as quickly as she could.

She closed his door softly behind them, and closed her eyes as she dropped the robe. She was afraid he wouldn't like what he saw.

Karlan looked her up and down, taking a step forward after a moment. He put his index finger under her chin and lifted it. He waited a moment for her to open her eyes, and when she did, he whispered, "You're beautiful. I'm glad you're my wife."

"You don't wish you'd chosen Chastity?"

He laughed. "Chris can deal with your nymphomaniac sister. I'm perfectly content with the woman I chose." He leaned down, kissing her softly. "Are you sure you're ready for this? Do you want to wait? I don't want to force you to do anything you're not ready for." He hoped she wouldn't take him up on his offer, but he felt the need to be kind after the way he'd exploded at her. He could forgive the vibrator, because he knew he was partially to blame.

She shook her head. "I'm sure I don't need more time. I wouldn't have asked for time three weeks ago, if I'd had a little time to get to know you first."

He smiled. "I had to make sure to stake my claim before my brothers saw you."

"I think your brothers are very content with my sisters." She reached out to him, moving her hands under the bottom of his T-shirt, stroking slowly up his chest. "We should get this off you."

He stepped back and stripped off his shirt, and she pressed up against him. "Do you have any idea how much your bare chest turns me on?"

"Not as much as your bare chest would turn me on," he quipped, grinned down at her. "Wanna compare?"

She swallowed hard. Part of making love was baring herself

for her husband. As hard as that was, she could do it. "Sure."

He blinked at her, surprised by her ready response. "Really?"

She nodded. "I think so."

"Are you nervous?"

"Of course, I'm nervous. I've never been with a man before."

No, just that ridiculous toy. "I'm not going to hurt you." He pushed one strap off her shoulder and down her arm, kissing a path from her cheek to her neck and down.

She wound her fingers through his hair, holding him to her. "That feels so nice!"

"Your skin is so soft!" His shorts were starting to constrict him too much, little Charlie pushing against the front of them. "Maybe we should take this to the bed."

At her nod, he scooped her up in his arms as if she weighed nothing, carrying her to the bed and gently laying her down on it. He quickly stripped off his shorts and followed her down.

Hope averted her eyes, not wanting to see him in all his glory. She knew they were married, but it didn't seem like something she should do. Her mother had talked about this being something only done in the dark. That meant she shouldn't look, right?

He looked down into her face. "You're allowed to look at me, you know. We're married."

"I know. Kind of."

"Kind of? What do you mean?"

"Promise you won't laugh?" How would she be able to explain her misgivings without sounding childish?

"If I laugh, you might leave. Or worse. Kick me out of my

own bed and make me sleep in that tiny little bed in your room."

"The guest room," she corrected.

"What?" Karlan asked.

"I'm sharing this room with you from now on. That's the guest room."

"Okay, I promise I won't laugh, and I'll leave it at that." Her rapid change of subject was starting to make his head spin, and he wanted to get this conversation over with so they could get to the good part of the evening.

"Well, my mom always made it sound like sex was dirty. She told me a woman never sees her husband naked, because it just isn't right."

He blinked a few times. "Seriously?"

"Seriously. I feel funny seeing you naked."

"So that's why you closed your eyes."

"Yeah." Hope made a face, more embarrassed than ever. "I know it's stupid, but we were raised in a very conservative, backwards, home. I plan on loving what we do together, but I have to get past my hang-ups to do that."

"We'll work through them together. What can I do to help?"

"For tonight, I think it's just a matter of...well, doing it." She couldn't even use one of his silly euphemisms now that the moment was upon them.

"Doing it? Doing what? Playing baseball?"

"Baseball?" she asked.

"I'm planning to hit a home run..."

Hope giggled a little. "I had no idea I married such a

romantic," she said, rolling her eyes.

"Hey, I'm trying to make sure you're in the mood here. Is it working?"

"Just looking at you puts me in the mood. No effort required." She pulled him down for a kiss, surprising him a little.

He kissed her with everything inside him. His tongue moved into her mouth to tangle with hers while his hands slowly stroked her garment off her body. When she was bare beneath him, he moved to her side, one hand going between her spread thighs to stroke her.

He kissed a trail from her lips down her neck and to her breast, taking one rosy peak into his mouth. "You taste good," he muttered against her flesh.

Hope had no idea what to do with her hands, so she wound them through his hair, arching up into his mouth. She focused on what he was doing to her, not on the feeling that what was happening was wrong. Knowing it wasn't wrong didn't seem to be enough for her. She had to block it out completely, forcing her mind to shut off, so she wouldn't feel guilty.

His hand between her thighs was stroking at her nub of flesh, making her heart beat rapidly. She felt out of breath, and a tightening was happening in her belly. She felt like something was going to break inside her. "I feel weird!"

He looked up at her, a twinkle in his eye. "What feels weird?" He caught her nipple between his lips again. "This?" He made his finger dance against the flesh between her thighs. "Or this?"

Her gasp at his movement between her thighs was all the answer he needed. He carefully plunged one finger inside of her, moving it slowly in and out of her tight channel.

She gasped, clutching his shoulders. "I don't think you should do that!" The tightening in her stomach was increasing, making her feel like she was going to explode. "You have to stop!"

He chuckled low in his throat. "Not on your life. Not 'til you finish."

"Finish? What do you mean?" Her mother had told her to lie back and let her husband do what he must. She couldn't have meant this. It felt too good! Suddenly her stomach clenched, and she let out a moan. She sank back into the pillows, feeling a little dazed. "Wow."

He laughed, moving to cover her with his body, pleased that he was finally getting a turn. "Wow? Is that all you can say?"

"More please?"

He pressed his lips to hers, slowly moving into her body. Her cry of pain caught him by surprise. "Are you all right?"

"I don't know. That hurt for a second, but I think I'm all right now."

He stared down at her, holding still within her. Something didn't seem right, but he was in too big of a hurry to worry about it just then. He started moving slowly within her, watching her face for further signs of pain. "How's that?"

"That feels nice." She wrapped her arms around him, stroking his bare back, scraping her fingernails on his skin.

He caught her legs and wrapped them around his waist, his

face buried against her throat. He was determined to make certain she found her pleasure again before he found his own.

Hope felt the now-familiar tightening in her belly start again, and she moved with him, wanting the same thing to happen that had happened before. She may not know much about how this was supposed to work, but she knew she liked everything she was feeling.

She broke apart in his arms minutes later, idly noting that he kept moving, until he shouted her name, collapsing atop her.

It took a few minutes for him to come back to earth, but he rolled to her side as soon as he realized where he was. "I'm sorry. I must have been crushing you."

Hope rolled with him, snuggling into his arms. "No, I liked it. I felt like I was part of you."

He stroked her cheek. "You're not allowed to move back to the spare bedroom now, just so you know. I'm keeping you right here where you belong."

She sighed happily. "I want to stay here. Then I won't have to keep hiding things from my sisters."

"Hiding things from your sisters?"

"You asked me to pretend we were intimate. My sisters wanted us to all take a pregnancy test together today. I took one, feeling like an idiot the whole time."

Karlan sighed. "Anyone pregnant?"

She nodded. "Two the first month. Terms of the will have been fulfilled."

"That was quick." He stroked his hand over her back.

She nodded, yawning. Looking at the clock, she groaned. "It's eleven. There aren't enough hours in the day."

"I caught you watching television tonight. It's the first time I've seen you really relax and stop working."

"I do know how to stop working. There just hasn't been a call for it yet. When we're sure we'll get to keep the ranch, I'll relax. Probably for a whole month."

He chuckled softly. "Go to sleep, Hope. Tomorrow is another busy day."

Her eyes were already drifting closed. "They always are."

Karlan kept his arms around her, cradling her against him. His wife was a special woman, one he already cared about more than he wanted to admit. How had he stayed angry with her for two weeks? He thought about the toy he'd found in her nightstand, and he knew it wasn't something she'd ever used. She'd been too surprised by her orgasm to be a regular sex toy user. But why did she have it?

He thought about waking her and asking her, but she was already asleep, her breathing even. He knew she was working as hard as he was to try to help keep the ranch. His mother had told him about how special she was, and how she seemed so sad at times, reading him the riot act.

"You've married a very special woman, Karlan James Culpepper. Don't you dare do anything to hurt her, or I'll buy the black-eyed peas myself!" she'd said. Karlan had no doubt she was referring to the country song, *Goodbye Earl*, where two women poisoned a man who had beaten one of them. His mother had said more than once if he ever hurt a girl that way, she'd make the black-eyed peas.

Of course, his mother had also told him and his brothers if they ever were out with a girl and just couldn't control themselves to call her and she'd bring a condom. Every time he'd thought he was going to make it into the backseat with a girl, he'd seen his mother's face swimming before his eyes. Talk about an erection killer.

She'd confessed a couple of years before that had been her intention all along. She'd wanted them to think of her. The woman was evil, devious, and brilliant, all rolled into one.

He yawned, adjusting Hope's head a little bit, so it wasn't cutting into his shoulder so much. He reached over and turned off the lamp beside the bed, doing his best not to disturb her. She worked too hard to not get enough sleep.

He fell asleep with a smile on his face, thinking about the long days and nights to come. His sweet little bride had obviously forgiven his craziness. Now, he just had to figure out what was up with the vibrator. And why had she let him be angry with her about it, instead of telling him she wasn't using the thing?

He shrugged. That was something they could figure out tomorrow, now that he knew they'd have one.

Chapter Ten

Hope woke up to Karlan's alarm going off at five the following morning. As much as she usually loved mornings, she let out a groan. She hadn't slept nearly enough.

Karlan rolled toward her, hugging her close. "Let's be late today."

She pulled back, looking at him in the darkness. "We can't be late. I have kids that will be at your mom's in two hours." She stifled a yawn. She wanted to stay in bed all day, but she had to take care of her responsibilities. No matter how much she didn't want to.

He sighed. "Adulting isn't easy."

She giggled, kissing him quickly. "No, it's not. But now that you're done with the traffic light nonsense, we'll have more time together in the evenings." She hoped he didn't have crises like that often, because she needed more time with him.

"But you're always sewing something in the evenings."

"Only because you're always on the phone. I've got most of the sewing I need to do caught up to the point I should be able to keep up during naptime." Was that why he hated her sewing machine? Because she spent so much time using it?

"Really? We're actually going to be able to act like

newlyweds and spend time together?"

"Really!" She rolled out of bed, hurrying to her robe. It was different seeing each other right before making love than it was the morning after. "I'll go make breakfast." She desperately needed another shower after the activities of the night before, but she'd get that after he left.

Over breakfast, she felt very shy, wondering if he was thinking about all the things they'd done together the night before. She was unable to meet his eyes directly. She knew they'd done nothing wrong, but she still felt strange in the daylight.

After they finished eating, he caught her to him, kissing her passionately. "Are you sure we can't be late today?"

"Do you really want to explain why you were late to Cooper? And your mother? Because I'm not explaining it. I love your mom, but I'm not talking about sex with my mother-in-law!"

He sighed. "I'm not afraid of telling Mom why we're late. It's Cooper that would scare me. That boy has us on a tighter schedule than I've ever dreamed a ranch would operate on. Why, even Granddaddy did whatever Cooper told him to do, because he knew the ranch would have folded without Cooper there to boss us all around." He kissed her one last time. "I'm looking forward to our evening together."

Hope clung to him for a moment. "Me too. How is it that we were married first, but got to spend time alone together last?"

"It's my stupid job as mayor. I enjoy it usually. I'll enjoy it again, I'm sure." He opened the door and turned to wink at her. "I'll see you at lunch time!"

She smiled, waving him off.

When she got to the big house, Joy hurried to her. "You look so happy!"

Hope smiled at her sister. "I am happy. Why wouldn't I be?"

Joy shrugged. "I'm not sure. But I've thought something was wrong for a while now." Joy was more in tune with Hope's emotions than her other sisters were. She hated that her sister sensed that she'd been unhappy.

"Nope. Life couldn't be better. How are you?"

Joy grinned, her whole face lighting up with the smile. "Joyful."

Hope laughed. Her sister had always been joyful. "I'm glad. Did you finish the castle?"

"Yes! It's up on eBay and already has ten bids!"

"Oh, that's great! What's your next project?" The Barbie castle had looked amazing the last time Hope had seen it, but that was the previous day. Hope couldn't wait to see it completely done.

"A snowmobile and condo. Should be fun!"

"Maybe you could make just some furniture sets as well. That would be a good break from the big projects." Hope grinned. "I'm thinking about taking tomorrow morning off. Could you cover for me?"

"Oh, definitely. Especially if it's for baby making purposes. We need as many babies around here as possible."

Hope blushed but didn't comment on why. "Thank you! I'll cover your naptime shift for you."

"Sounds good to me." Joy smiled as Faith came into the big house. "We weren't expecting you today!"

Faith held up a piece of paper. "Hope, we've sold all but five of your sets of holiday outfits. I need you to make more! That was a brilliant idea."

"How about orders for the babies? Have you gotten more?"

"Yes! I got four overnight. I can't keep up!" Faith smiled at Hope. "I also got a special request from a mother who purchased a baby doll for her daughter last year."

"What's that?"

"Her daughter wants a dress to match her dolls. Because it's a custom order, we could charge double what we usually would." Faith bit her lip, waiting for Hope's response.

"Sure. I can do that." Hope frowned. "I'll have to look online to find some good matching patterns. How specific were they about what they wanted?"

"The mom wants an everyday dress for them both. She doesn't want something fancy, because that would be too much work to keep nice."

Hope smiled. "Good, that won't take as long to make either. Tell her we'll do it, and I'll start looking for patterns. Do you have the little girl's size?"

"Six."

"All right. I'm on it."

Faith hugged Hope and hurried back out the door, obviously going to work on making more baby dolls. It was nice to see her able to work without censure. "We're never going to be able to keep up with her rapid orders," Hope told Joy.

Linda walked in then. "Faith got more orders? Those dolls of hers are amazing!"

"Lots more orders." Hope turned to face her mother-in-law. "Joy is going to work for me tomorrow morning. I'm taking the morning off."

Linda smiled. "I think that's a really good idea. You've worked non-stop seven days per week since you got here."

"So have you!"

"Well, that's different." Linda shrugged. "I'm used to working all the time."

"And you had houseguests for much longer than anyone should have houseguests. And you've opened your house up to fifteen kids running wild every day."

"But it's fun!"

Hope shook her head. "If you really don't mind, then I'm going to do it."

"Good for you. I hate seeing you girls work so hard to try to save the ranch."

"It's our children's inheritance." Hope had believed that when she first arrived, and now she believed it again. Of course, she and Karlan hadn't exactly talked about their future. What if he was still planning on ending their marriage in eleven months like he'd said?

She shook her head. She wasn't going to worry about it. That was the whole point of taking the next morning off work. She would be able to talk to Karlan about her worries.

When he came in for lunch, he kissed her sweetly. She stood on tiptoe to whisper in his ear, "Joy is going to take care of the kids for me in the morning. Tell Cooper you're taking the morning off, and we'll have our own private little honeymoon."

Karlan grinned. "I'll tell him this afternoon."

*****

After she got home that evening, she put a chicken pot pie she'd made over the weekend into the oven. She needed to talk to Karlan before anymore hanky-panky took place. She had to know what her future would hold.

While she waited for him, she picked up the house, making sure it was in perfect order. She was a little embarrassed she hadn't made the bed before going to work that morning. It was so unlike her to neglect her responsibilities that way.

The potpie was on the table when he opened the door. "That smells good," he said. "Have I told you lately that you're a wonderful cook?"

She smiled, shaking her head. "No, but I'm glad you think so." While they ate, she told him about the outfits that had sold for Faith's business. Now that Faith had finally come clean about what she was doing, it was easier for Hope to talk about it. She hated keeping secrets from her husband. "You know all those little outfits I made for Faith's dolls?"

He nodded. "Yeah, you worked on them night and day."

"I made twenty-two sets of six outfits, and we've sold all but five of them. I need to start making more. Isn't that great?"

"I guess. Are you really making a profit on those?"

"Oh, yeah! It costs us fourteen dollars and fifty cents to make six outfits, and we're selling them for seventy-five bucks for the set of six. That's over sixty dollars profit for each set of clothes."

"And how much time are you putting into a set of six?"

"Less than I thought. It takes me about fifteen minutes to sew each outfit, now that I have it down, and I cut them all out together. I spend around six hours cutting out twenty-two of every outfit. So when all the math is done, I'm making around thirty-five dollars per hour. That's really good money."

He nodded. "Very good. That's going to help our bottom line a lot."

"I don't think you have any idea. I've started a savings account for our contributions, and we're going to be able to make a significant difference." She looked at him. "We haven't really talked about money, because I didn't feel like I could approach you with the way things were between us. How much do you think it's going to cost to pay Travis off?"

Karlan rubbed the back of his neck. "Well, the buildings aren't part of his inheritance. The big house was left to Mom. Each of our homes were left to us. It's really just the land that we'll need to pay him for. And his share of the cattle of course."

"How much do you think that equates to?"

"His share of the land would be about a hundred grand. Another eighty-grand for his share of the herd. In my head, I'm rounding up to two-hundred fifty thousand. I don't think he can ask for more than that."

Hope's face lit up. "We can do that!"

"We can?"

She nodded. "Definitely. It'll be tight for six months, but after that, we're good."

"But can you keep it up for six months? All of you? I know the pace is pretty hard."

She laughed. "If you men can keep it up for six months, we can keep it up for six months. We're strong women."

He smiled at that. "I know you are."

"Knowing we're helping so much with our crafts, are you still jealous of my sewing machine?"

He stared at her with a blank look. "Your sewing machine? Why would I be jealous of your sewing machine?"

She frowned. "I have no idea. You told me you were though!"

"I did?" Karlan had no idea what she was talking about.

"You said you were jealous of my machine." Hope said.

His eyes widened. "You thought I meant your sewing machine? No! I meant your vibrator!" Why would any man ever be jealous of a sewing machine?

"My—" She blushed scarlet. "Chastity gave me that for a wedding gift. I didn't want to hurt her feelings, but I would never use it!" She leaned close to him to whisper conspiratorially. "I think it was made for an elephant. That thing is huge!"

He laughed. "Yeah, it is. Why do you still have it then?"

"I didn't want to throw it away and have you accidentally see it. I had visions of you taking the trash out, and the bag busting, and that huge thing coming out! I was planning on taking it with me when I go grocery shopping this week and putting it in a dumpster somewhere." Her eyes narrowed at him. "You mean that's what you've been upset with me about?"

He nodded. "I thought you were refusing to have sex with me and using a vibrator instead. It was more than a little annoying."

Hope frowned. "I guess I can see that. You should have just asked about it. I put it in a drawer because Chastity gave it to me right before the wedding, and I had no idea what to do with the thing!"

"Your sister is a mess."

Hope nodded. "She definitely is. She would be mortified if she knew it had caused problems between us, though. She gave it to me in case you were bad in the sack. Her words, not mine."

"Well, throw the blasted thing away. I promise you, if you ever need a sex toy, I'm here for you!"

Hope blushed. "I will gladly throw it away. I felt like an idiot having it hidden in my drawer all this time anyway." She reached out and took his hand. "I should have made sure to clarify when you were upset about my machine. I really thought you meant my sewing machine, and I thought you were nuts. And when you told me you wouldn't stay married to me…"

"I never should have said that. I didn't mean it, even then. I was tired and angry but saying that was inexcusable. I always knew we'd work it out!"

"I didn't. I kept envisioning my future alone. I knew I loved you as soon as you said we were splitting. I don't know what's wrong with me that it hit me then, but it did!"

"Wait. You love me?" Karlan pulled her from her chair and onto his lap. "You really love me?"

She nodded. "Of course, I do. I knew I loved you when I knew I wanted to make love with you."

"I love you too, Hope. I hate that we wasted so much time."

"We got to know each other better. How is that time wasted?"

He kissed her softly. "I guess it's not, but it feels like it is."

"I'm glad we talked about this. Now we don't have to waste time talking tomorrow. We can skip right to the good stuff."

"We can skip right to the good stuff now…"

She giggled. "You go get a shower, and I'll have the dishes done by the time you're done. I'll meet you in bed!"

"We could shower together…"

"We could…"

"Fine, get the dishes done and meet me in bed. You'll just sneak out of bed in the middle of the night to get them done anyway!"

Hope grinned at him. "You already know me so well. I'll race you to see who's done first!"

He kissed her one last time before heading to the bedroom. "You'd better hurry!"

Of course, I'll hurry. I have everything I want. A man who loves me and a good life. Moving to Culpepper, Wyoming, was the smartest thing she'd ever done!